Running Shadow

CATHLEEN ELLIS

Running Shadow
Copyright © 2019 Cathleen Ellis
www.CathleenEllis.com

Cover design by Launie Parry
Interior design by Brian Schwartz

ISBN: 978-1629671734
Library of Congress Control Number: 2020903921

YOUNG PEOPLE IN LOVE
IN THE HEARTLAND OF AMERICA

OTHER BOOKS BY
CATHLEEN ELLIS

www.CathleenEllis.com

A Scarf of Promise

Just Let It Go

Castle in the Air

Tend My Flowers

Making Our Way

Together Now

Kara's Love

Sky Tossed

Baskets on Christmas Lane

A Humble Task

Up To Me

What's Beneath

Christmas Bright

Loving Presence

A Voice for Gabby

Shadow to Sunshine

Love Ties

Carry Me On

Roses for Meredith

Future Bright Light

Old Crooked Road

Compass North

1

August 2007

"Hey, why'd your family give property to the Land Trust?"

"Cole, Cami's already told you," Justine bumped his shoulder.

"Oh, yeah, has to do with taxes, by donating it."

"That's right," Cami turned back to look at them.

They hurried along the path they created two years ago. It took them to their play campsite.

"Yeah, we can play here, always. The donated property, with the Land Trust," Cami paused, "it'll be aways from right here, along the fence line that's near the edge of the property. Dad did this to protect the land, and hoped it would be a recreational opportunity, maybe a trail someday, for folks."

"That makes sense; your family never uses this beautiful area."

"Dad always called it his forest reserve. But no, my folks never used it, just the three of us. We've had our picnics and hide and seek fun, a chance to sit and talk, these past years. Guys, mom's sick, finally admitted that the pain pills she got when she broke her leg," she paused, "well."

Her voice trailed off, unable to say anymore.

"Yeah, my doctor dad says it's a dilemma every time he prescribes a medication. He warns his patient, about when there's an addictive part."

"Yeah, Cole, well, mom she's addicted."

She shifted her gaze from friend to friend as tears welled up in her eyes. Justine and Cole flinched at her sadness. They put their gear down at their play campsite and sat down.

"I'm just so glad I have you two in my life. Mom did the right thing getting your mom to be our housekeeper, Justine. She's kinda taught mom how to cook; I'm glad Indella prepares our meals. You're my friend and companion because of that. You've helped me learn about the housework, that you help your mom with at our home. And Cole, my pal friend, just right next door," she touched his upper arm.

They both nodded to Cami.

"Mom told me that about six months ago, Cami, about the addiction. She's been watchin' over Priscilla for a long time."

"Guys, how come I never noticed, about my mom?"

"Hey, girl, your mom's got you going every day of the week with some activity or other. She's either takin' you to practice for dance, or singing, or gymnastics, or acting, or piano, or karate, and now you've just finished up a woodcarving class."

"And church, at least you get to relax at church on Sunday."

"Justine, mom and dad haven't gotten me to church; Aunt Bea's kinda taken over the religious part."

"Uh huh, we come and sit with you at church now, 'cause you're comin' again. Aunt Bea always saves plenty of room, so we can scoot in."

"Confirmation wasn't that long ago for us," Cole added.

"Right."

"School's gonna start in a week. This'll be our last time out here, at least for a while."

"It's OK, I got soccer at Hillyer."

"I got spirit team at Hillyer," said Cami.

"And I'm in spirit team at Ephrine High."

"Let's get our little bridge, a covering over the stream, finished. We promised ourselves to do it, so next year, we won't get our feet wet trying to cross in the spring."

They set to work with their hammers and nails. They brought the wood for the small bridge several weeks before, sawed it, and stored it away from the water. Within an hour they set the wood covering over the stream. They stood, readjusting the covering, securing it with rocks so it wouldn't slide from side to side.

"Your birthday picnic in your backyard, it was nice."

"Yeah, 'zactly what I wanted, just you two."

"Unbelievable, Cami, you just turned 14, but a sophomore like us," Justine shook her head to her.

"Very tall, matured early, like my tall parents; they figured I needed to be in kindergarten at 3 years of age. I could already read and do math, knew my multiplication tables."

"So that kinda explains your age and the grade you're in."

"Dudes, the covering over the stream works great now. But then," Cole paused, giving the girls a pained look.

"Yeah, we know," Justine grimaced, "until the area gets flooded, from the rains, then, well, we don't know what'll happen."

"Hey, we'll just check on it next spring," Cami smiled to her friends.

They nodded.

"Sheez, gotta head back, this took longer than I thought; I got soccer practice," Cole stood after they had their water and candy bars.

They walked back to Cami's, through the back yard and around to the front of her stately two-story home. They all saw, counting two Ephrine police cars, one county sheriff vehicle, and Aunt Bea's red pickup.

They dropped their gear. Cole stood between the two girls and held on tight to them as they approached the front of the home.

"We love each other, no matter what, ladies."

"No matter what," Justine echoed, in a whisper.

Cami watched her aunt, standing straight and tall, her lips thin and her eyes empty. The three young people also stood straight and tall, waiting for her to speak.

Bea shook her head as she walked toward them from the front porch steps, "Their private plane went down a minute after takeoff for the trip back, some terrible problem."

They all knew Gilbert and Priscilla took a trip to the West Virginia mountains with their friends. After that trip Priscilla planned to go into rehab.

Bea put her arms around all three teens as they broke into sobs. They stood together for a time. Cami started the Lord's Prayer, and they all joined in.

Cole's dad and Justine's mom stood nearby. Bea loosened her hold on the three of them. Justine went to her mom, and Cole walked toward his dad. They exchanged words and hugs. Then they all moved toward Cami and Bea.

"We'll stay a little while, help out," Indella spoke as she nodded to Justine, Bea and Cami.

"Whatever we can do; we're right next door," Cole gazed at Cami.

"That's right," added his dad.

She watched Cole's face remain ashen and his eyes blank. She nodded. Cami and Justine held hands after they grabbed their gear they set down. They walked into the beautiful home. Indella followed, holding Bea by her shoulder.

"Want company?" Justine asked before Cami went upstairs to her bedroom to brush out her hair, sweaty from working on the bridge

"Nah, I'll be down in a little while, unpacking my stuff up here. I'm in shock; totally numb; I'm not understanding what's happened."

Justine burst into tears after she watched Cami walk slow, holding the hand rail, until she got to the top of the stairs. Justine hurried to the kitchen where her mom held her and rocked her back and forth.

Cami brushed out her shiny brown hair with its natural auburn streaks. She put away everything from her backpack except for the food and tools she would take back downstairs. Then she knelt down, holding two pictures in frames that she kept at her bedside table, a recent one of her parents from one of their trips, and the other of Priscilla and her. She remembered she caught people by surprise; how she looked like her mom, size-wise, tall and slim, same eyes, but her mom was a natural blonde.

"Mom and dad, I'm thinkin' you'll be home soon, to hug me and tell me about your trip. You two are in my heart, and in my memory, have been, are now, and will forever be. God, I gotta help Aunt Bea; she looks beyond sad, a worried look in her eyes the last few times she's come by to see us. Yeah, she's been comin', kinda unannounced, when she's not at the lawyer's office. And 'course, she's doing church with me.

And God, I'll stand with you; please be by my side, be beside me   It's gonna be bad, I'm gonna need you, when it finally hits me, what's happened. Mom, you've helped me stand on my own, since you shared with me your addiction and coming rehab. You knew I could handle it. And I've got this, I promise."

The four of them sat at the big kitchen island, having salad and sandwiches, an early dinner. Aunt Bea wanted them to talk with her after they ate. Justine and Cami cleaned up the kitchen. Indella poured a small glass of wine for Bea and her. The girls drank a combination ice tea/lemonade.

"Here's the big picture, ladies," Aunt Bea teared up, cleared her throat and began. "The NTSB will investigate this crash; we might know something about the cause by the holidays. I'm seeing those questioning eyes, girls. The NTSB is the National Transportation and Safety Board. It's a job of theirs, to work on plane crashes, what caused them."

She watched the teens nod to her.

"Indella, you've shared that you've been paid through the end of August, correct?"

"Right, Priscilla always paid me ahead, the first of the month for the month I would work."

"We'll have to let you go, maybe help out here for a week. I'm so sorry, so much stuff's gotta happen at this home. I'll have to ask you to gather the things you've kept here in the next several days. Gilbert's completely broke, lost everything in the stock market mess of this year. And, he hadn't been paying the property taxes on this home, or the land, and a lot of other debt."

"Aunt Bea, what about the Land Trust, the land he gave to them?"

"Since he deeded the land to that nonprofit, it belongs to the Trust." She nodded her head to them, "Thank goodness, that was one smart thing he did with some of the property."

"So, we need to sell the house, to pay off debt, right?"

"That's correct, you're moving to my home, Cami. It's just a week to the start of school."

"We'll go now, Bea," Indella and Justine rose and hugged them both before they left.

"You're in our thoughts and prayers," Justine nodded to them as they walked away from Bea and Cami sitting at the kitchen island.

"Can't afford Hillyer, Aunt Bea, you need to take me to register for Ephrine High. And we'll need to let Hillyer know I won't be returning."

"Tomorrow, that's on my list for tomorrow."

Cami felt like gentle waves splashed over her body, moving her forward to some great unknown. She looked over and above her aunt's head, thinking and thinking, a swirl wrapping around her head.

"No more spirit team."

"That's right, at least not at Hillyer, but, remember Ephrine High, Justine, she's on their spirit team, since last year. Maybe, well, hang in there, with your dance, and gymnastics training, who knows."

Bea looked directly into Cami's green eyes, same eyes as her mom's, same eye color.

"I can tell you're thinkin' through all this; I'm proud of you, Cami. We gotta take it one day at a time."

They heard the doorbell ring. Aunt Bea went to the door and ushered in a tall and disheveled young man.

"Cami, oh Cami," he strode toward her as she stood up and came to him.

"I'm a mess, just came from the soccer field; Cole missed practice. But he came by to talk to coach about his missing most of practice, and to me about your folks, I'm just in shock."

Alex watched Cami stare at him with unseeing eyes.

"Whatever I can do, to help, please let me know, spend time with you, like I've been these past months. Would you like that?"

"Aunt Bea, tell him please."

"Alex, Cami'll be at Ephrine High for the rest of her high school career. Her dad lost everything, in the stocks he'd invested in. Family debts gotta be paid; house and land and possessions sold, like right away."

Alex stepped away from Cami.

He shook his head to her, "Cami, where'll you go, oh dear God, what's gonna happen to you?"

Cami watched tears spurt in his eyes. He wiped them away with his hands and then onto his soiled soccer shorts.

"Aunt Bea's taking me in. You know dad and Aunt Bea's parents are dead, and mom's folks live overseas, missionaries in Africa. Starting tomorrow, her home will be mine, thank you, Aunt Bea. Everything you see, Alex," she looked at her aunt, "is gonna be gone, estate sale."

Alex stepped to Cami and held her close.

"Thanks for stopping by, Alex," she nodded to him.

He took a step away from her, "You're important, to your aunt, to me, to your friends. Please take care of yourself," he let out a big sigh as he looked at her, "time, Cami. "

∽

Mrs. Hampter watched Cami sit up straight, her back not touching the chair back.

"Cami, you've forgotten, I plan to continue to see you once a month for a while longer."

A small smile appeared on Cami's face as she nodded to her school counselor. She tried to relax as she slid until her back touched the chair.

"So that's why you've called me in."

Mrs. Hampter nodded to her, "It's almost Christmas, how's your readjusting going?"

Cami shook her head as she looked around the counselor's office.

"Whew, the numbness, my brain fog, is less, anger pretty much gone; unbelievable resentment still gets me upset. I was one super-privileged, spoiled, rich kid, arrogant brat. I live in the real world now. I'm learnin' how to work, at her home, and in her small yard. Aunt Bea, what an awesome and wonderful woman she is, so totally the person I want to become one day. She moved here two years ago, has a great job as a paralegal in a large lawyer's office in Ephrine. She bought a townhome as soon as she got here. I can't believe she could ever have been my dad's little sister. She has so much perseverance, initiative, and together we're moving forward with all the duties involved in surviving loved ones, their dying."

"Would you like to share?"

Cami nodded and leaned forward holding up her index finger.

"First thing, my parents' debts cleared; house, vehicles and property sold, estate is almost closed."

She paused, thought for a moment and then continued.

"The thing that scared me the most, debt. It took these months since August. One good bit of news, mom had a life insurance policy with me as beneficiary."

"That's super, Cami, your aunt, you can help her with your room and board."

"And my university education, I'll have enough to make it through the four year with scholarships I'm gonna apply for, but I got to help her budget my money. Under a different set of circumstances, I coulda ended up homeless, in a foster home. I'm so lucky; I'm so blessed."

Her smiling green eyes shone into her counselor's as she nodded.

"You may be eligible for HOPE, with your great GPA, and if you decide to stay in Georgia for university."

"Yes, that too."

"School, how's it going?"

"Classes and grades, dropped, then I picked grades up the last few weeks; I love calc, and my AP classes. Once in a while I still have trouble concentrating on what I'm doing. Everyone says it's part of the grieving process. The D class after school here at Ephrine's been helpful. I was in it for several weeks early in the school year. I had no idea so many of the students had situations, kinda like mine, kids with mostly divorce going on, a couple others with losses, but not like me, both parents. And Mrs. Hampter," Cami stopped and smiled to her counselor, "you've helped me plan; I'll spend part of my school day senior year at Humphrey University taking classes."

"So extracurricular, and may I ask, you and Justine?"

"Justine and I're super close. And you know what, Mrs. Hampter, my richy rich friends at Hillyer," Cami stopped and lowered her eyes, shaking her head.

"Yes?"

They've dropped me like I have some disease."

"Oh?"

Cami raised her eyes to her counselor and began laughing, "Some disease, called being poor, without a bunch of money."

"They weren't friends, Cami," Mrs. Hampter gave her a serious look, her lips pursed in a thin line.

Cami nodded, somber now, "They certainly were not, but that's so devastating when I realized what happened, what having money can mean."

They sat in silence for a moment.

Cami nodded, "One friend remains, Cole, still at Hillyer."

"Weren't you, he and Justine best friends?"

"That's right, and still are, best friends from a long time ago. Cole's family was neighbors to my family at my old place. His family's got money, but he's sincere, and I believe he'll help me get through all this."

"Extracurricular, as I asked earlier?"

"I'm not in any of the classes I used to take after school and weekends, all the dance and stuff, but I still practice everything I've learned, including all the gymnastics. I'm thinkin' of trying out for Ephrine's spirit team in the spring, when I'm feeling more secure about my future. One of the killer things I had to do was let go of my spirit team uniforms from Hillyer Academy. I bawled like a baby. Aunt Bea suggested I give the uniform parts I could, that didn't say Hillyer, to a nonprofit clothing store. I did that and it made me feel better, that someone maybe could use my stuff."

"This holiday season, plans?"

"Midnight mass, of course, Aunt Bea's invited Justine, and Justine's mom, Indella, for Christmas dinner, early Tuesday afternoon. Merry Christmas, Mrs. Hampter, to you and your family, I appreciate everything you've done for me, way beyond what I ever expected."

"I'm here for you; all of you students, it's my job, and with you, my pleasure."

Cami saw her wide smile as she handed her a card and then left the counselor's office.

Sheree Hampter opened the card, saw the snowy winter scene on the card's outside and read the inside. It was all in Cami's handwriting.

Mom and Dad thank you for helping me. Yes, they're still with me, in my heart, and in my mind, a vision standing next to me, alongside God. Love, Cami

A sob escaped Sheree's throat. She put her head down on her desk and cried.

ᏸ

Cami stood in the living room, gazing at the tree Aunt Bea asked her to decorate. They found the tree together, at a little tree stand outside of town. It got marked down, being so close to Christmas. Cami had 10 family ornaments Aunt Bea let her have before the estate sale. She gathered them close to her and sat down before she started the decorating.

"The angel, Cole gave to me when I was 11; it's my favorite."

She held the small angel in her hand, a delicate porcelain piece. She thought back to September when she asked him to go with her to get the necklace appraised. As they rode their bikes to the recommended jewelry store, she shared with Cole.

"Please, just between us, mom gave me this, a gift, that in a note she said she got from a friend. I learned about it when the estate opened up her safety deposit box. The gift was in an envelope with a letter inside that mom had notarized. It said that the contents were a gift for me on the date mom wrote down. Also enclosed in that envelope was an appraisal of the jewelry, at that time. Finally, mom wrote I would get the gift when she felt I was responsible enough to take care of it."

"Oh my gosh, Cami, it was never intended for you to get it."

"To get it now, Cole, at my age, I'm sure she meant when I was a lot older."

He nodded to her, "A course, years from now, right?"

"Right, but that time's come. I'll put it in my own safety deposit box at the bank, once I know."

"Got it, once it's appraised, then you can sell it, when the time comes, when you need the money, you know, like for college, or after that."

"That's it."

"On our way home, I think you're strong enough now to know what I saw happening at your home, a few years ago." He paused for a moment, thinking. He turned to her, "Hey, do you trust that jewelry store, and the appraiser?"

"I do, Cole, it was the estate lawyer who told me the store was honest, and would give me a good appraisal. They'd used the store before for appraisals."

After working with the jewelry store's appraiser, they left with a receipt for the possible appraisal cost. The appraiser would call Cami once a value could be placed on the piece of jewelry.

"Tell me, we're riding back to Aunt Bea's."

"An older man, owner of lots of horses in this area, well, while your dad was gone on his many trips away, he visited your mom. I often saw his big rig parked in your driveway."

"Yeah," Cami looked over to him as they rode side by side, "they went riding together."

"And Cami, he was there, during school days, when you weren't home."

"Uh huh, I suspected that. And I gotta stop for a minute, let's pull over to this grassy area."

Cami sobbed as she sat next to Cole. He held her close. In a little while she stopped crying and wiped her eyes and nose.

"I think you know this, Cole, 'cause we've talked, mom was pregnant with me, just turned 17, when she and dad got married.'

"Oh my gosh, I didn't realize they were that young."

"Mom was a senior, didn't graduate."

She turned to him and shook her head, "Dad wasn't her first love affair, she told me once, about two other guys, before him."

She put her head on her knees and stopped talking.

Cami turned and looked into his dark blue eyes, "It's not our place to judge."

"That's right," Cole nodded to her.

She heard the firm tone of his voice. They got back on their bikes and rode the distance to Aunt Bea's driveway.

As he walked her to the door, she spoke out, "Me and Justine, we've decided, no screwing with any guy. It's gotta be making love with someone we love and care about, have gotten to know, when we're a lot older."

He hugged her and moved back. She saw his eyes, serious now.

"But the hormones, they're pretty strong."

"Yeah, but I'm stronger," she smiled to him as he got on his bike and started to ride away. He looked back as she waved to him. He waved back.

∞

Cami shook herself from her remembrance of that September time. She got up and strung colored lights on the four foot tree, starting from the top and winding the string around. Then she hung her precious ornaments plus five that Aunt Bea asked her to place on the tree, her aunt's special ornaments.

"I need to go write in my journal 'cause I'm feeling sad, blue, missing mom and dad."

She walked up the steps to her bedroom, down the hall from her aunt's. She grabbed her journal from the tiny white desk and sat on the floor writing.

12/24/07 *Mom, you always told me, Cami, make the best of this day you have before you. I'm trying my best, mom.*

She stopped writing and looked over to a small white bookcase she got to bring from her old bedroom. Then she wrote.

Dad, I'm looking at two projects sitting on my top shelf you helped me with, a Lego space vehicle, and an Erector set ferris wheel with crank motor that actually makes the ferris wheel go. We had so much fun doing the work; it's my favorite memory of spending time with you.

She laid her head against the side of the bed. "And dad," she thought, "I really think I'll be an engineer one day." She wrote *I read all kinda stuff about bridges, and building big buildings, and wind stress, and geological surveys of underground contents. I miss you mom, and I miss you dad. Merry Christmas. Down here on earth, it's a time of caring, a time of peace.*

She put away her journal in its special spot on the first shelf of her bookcase.

೫

"It's been so great for you to have this special dinner with us."

"You're a good cook, Bea, the turkey breast, so juicy and tender."

"Why thank you, Justine," Bea smiled to her and looked over to Indella, "your mom, she's one outstanding cook. I'm just so pleased that you're employed at Ephrine Memorial, in the kitchen, with benefits, that's so wonderful."

"I'm going to be the assistant chef, fancy name for assistant cook. The registered dietician, well, she's such a huge help, with all the various diets, that our patients have."

Cami watched Indella beam to them, her dark brown eyes sparkling.

"If stuff hadn't happened to me and my family, you'd still be working for us. This's been a fabulous opportunity for you."

"It has been; it's just so sad about the circumstances. How're you doing, Cami?"

"Peaks and valleys, but things are smoothing out, wouldn't you say so, Aunt Bea?"

"Yes, much's happened. Cami's a lot stronger young lady, bridged from the old life to her new one. And so am I, much stronger, unbelievable how folks can cope, and even thrive, when tough times happen."

"You're right, Bea," Indella nodded to them, "but, well Priscilla."

Bea spoke up, "You can take this, Cami, your mom, toxic."

"I know that, Aunt Bea, but after I was born," she became silent.

"Yes, she took the responsibility for you very seriously. It changed her for the better."

Indella smiled to Cami, "Yes, my dear, I can vouch for that. But I had to nudge her along, the learning to cook simple stuff, the laundry, caring for the house, baby steps."

"Ah, baby steps," Cami echoed.

They all laughed.

Cami and Justine cleared the dining room table and brought coffee for the four of them.

"Dessert?"

"Let's wait a few minutes."

"Justine, have you told Aunt Bea about spirit team, how it's going?"

"Nope," she paused and looked around at them, "it's crazy busy with my school work, and team practice two afternoons a week, for at least an hour and a half."

"And you have games where you participate?"

"Yes, that also, soccer and football, afternoon and night performing."

"Cami, do you think you might want to try out?"

"Absolutely, Aunt Bea, Hillyer's spirit team that I was on as a freshman, it was super busy with practices and games, exactly like Justine says. I would like to do that again."

"So, girls, tell me just what spirit team is. You're not cheerleaders, right?"

"That's right, we're more performers, dancers and gymnasts, do everything to music."

"Oh, so the cheerleaders do just that, lead cheers?" Bea asked.

Justine added, "They're terrific dancers, gymnasts, like us, except they use their voices."

"Aunt Bea, the spirit team extends out the school spirit and the camaraderie of all the students. You outa come to a football game next season. It's really awesome, the show that's put on during half time, the band, cheerleaders, spirit team, all working together."

"Oh Bea," Justine added, "we also perform at basketball games, and for wrestling matches, and special times when a school group gets honored."

Justine stopped talking and started to tear up.

"But Bea, if it hadn't been for Priscilla, I would never've gotten to be on a spirit team."

"How's that, honey, are you OK?"

"No, I'm not," Justine sobbed for a time, looking around to them, "I'm thinking of your mom, Cami. All those years, from the time I was little and first came with mom to your home, Priscilla insisted that I participate with you. So I learned to dance, to do gymnastics and ballet and to sing, and do acting, and horseback riding. And I loved it all."

Justine grabbed her mom's hand and Cami's hand and squeezed them.

Indella spoke up, "My daughter and I, blessed beyond measure to have Cami and her parents in our lives. Gilbert and Priscilla paid for everything for Justine, all the classes through the years, and I'm so appreciative."

Cami watched everyone's smiles.

"Pumpkin pie, with whipped topping, for everyone?"

"Yes, plus coffee refills, please, Cami."

Justine helped her bring the pie on the plates to the table.

"Thought you could put on your own topping; see how you like it. I baked it myself, uh, ready made pie crust, and I followed the directions on the can of pumpkin pie mix."

She poured coffee for them all.

"Hope it tastes OK," Cami thought, "I'm in uncharted waters with pie."

"Uuummm, very tasty, Cami," Indella said, "Just enough cinnamon, ginger, and cloves, and a little brown sugar."

"Thanks, I just put in a little more than the recipe suggested, 'cause to me it tasted blah."

"Well done, we might need to have second helpings of pie," Bea smiled to Cami as they all giggled.

℘

New Year's Eve day Cami had a surprise. Aunt Bea worked only that morning at the law office. She brought in the mail. Cami got home from a bike ride with Justine.

"Fun to get out today?"

"Great, Aunt Bea, Justine, me, well, we're really glad to see this year over. It's been, the most difficult one, so far, for me."

"You have a letter."

"Me?"

"Uh huh, from overseas."

Cami opened the envelope with care, not disturbing the strange return address or the colorful stamp. She looked over the outside of the card, a different-looking holiday card. Inside she saw a folded paper and the handwriting on the card, *your grandparents, the Standin's.*

"Aunt Bea, it's a card from my grandparents in Africa. I'm taking it up to my room. I'll read the note."

"Good, Cami, take your time," Aunt Bea gave her a concerned look and kissed her on her forehead.

Cami put away her bike helmet in the hall closet and went to her room. The brain fog she experienced early on after her parents' deaths came back for a little while. She closed her eyes and let the waves of grief flow over her. As her eyes cleared from crying she remembered Priscilla sharing with Cami her own teenage story.

"I despised my parents, dad, the preacher, and mom, the preacher's wife. Yeah, I was a preacher's kid. And I misbehaved, a lot. As soon as I knew I was pregnant, I told Gilbert and our parents. My parents disowned me, on the spot, told me to pack a bag and get out. The next day I married Gilbert and left my family home, well, it was the happiest day of my life. I would be with the man I loved. A month later my folks took over the Uganda church. It was a dream they had for many years. When I married, their dream came to be. I got what I wanted, and they got what they wanted."

Cami blew out a breath, "Never met these folks, only pictures, a letter once or twice that mom always shared with me. Mom wrote, sent pictures as I grew up. I wonder, what do they want?"

2

Cami read the letter through several times. She took it and the card downstairs where her aunt sat at the small kitchen island.

Cami placed the letter near her aunt.

"I'm fixing myself a cup, want more coffee?"

"Thanks, yes, sure it's OK for me to read this?"

"Absolutely."

As Cami had, Bea read the letter over several times.

They looked at each other, shaking their heads.

"After almost 15 years, they want to see you, Cami. You are their granddaughter. And you are, well, not Priscilla."

Cami laughed at her aunt's tone after she said that.

"You're such a fine young person, Cami, I'm so proud of you. And what you've accomplished, with a solid, common sense head on your shoulders, well, they'll be very happy."

What Cami and Bea read was in February the Standin family would be residents of a Georgia community. Their mother church called them back to take over a small, failing church that they would try to resurrect from losing more church members along with the church building's structural issues. Their town was three hours from Ephrine.

"That's good, I'll finally get to meet them. Besides you, they're my family, all that I've got."

"Right," Bea nodded to her.

"Gosh, I know nothing about them, not their birthday month and day, not anything."

"This'll give you a chance to get acquainted. You're gonna mend a lot of fences, that your mom put up in front of them and her. Consider this as a present, getting to know folks to replace your own folks."

"Present and a challenge, oh my gosh, Aunt Bea, that reminds me, the appraisal, of the necklace my mom gave to me as a gift."

"You've picked it up from the jewelry store?"

"Yes, yesterday, I hadn't had time to go there until our Christmas break. I rode my bike, took it directly from the appraiser at the jewelry store to my personal safety deposit box at our bank, where I put it for safe keeping, along with the paper indicating the appraised value of the necklace right now. The appraiser'll bill me after the first of the year for his time. He apologized for taking so long to get back to me. He said his holiday business, crazy busy."

"That's good; we'll need to look at your budget again, Cami."

"Right and add $50,000 to the budget; that was the appraisal. With proper planning all my college's covered, and something for my someday."

"Goodness, I had no idea, oh my gosh, Cami."

Cami shook her head to her aunt, "That friend cared a great deal for my mom."

Bea fell silent, unable to say a word.

❧

Cami decided to send a Christmas card to her grandparents. At the bottom of the card she wrote:

"Once you get settled in your home here in the US I hope I will one day get to meet you. Be safe returning to our country. Cami

She just finished writing the note at her small desk when she heard her aunt calling her. She stepped out in the hall as Aunt Bea asked her to come down.

"You've a guest."

Cami bounded down the steps and stopped as she stepped on the last one. Ahead she saw a tall short-haired blonde young man.

"Cole, oh my gosh, it's been so long."

They moved to each other. He handed her a single red rose bud wrapped in greenery and tied with a green ribbon. She accepted it and came to him, lifting her arms to hug him. They held on.

He whispered, "It's been so long; I'm sorry, Cami. Stuff's just interfered. But I wanted to see you. And it's almost 2008, a happier new year, it's sure to be."

"I'm certainly hoping," she stepped away from him, "thank you for the beautiful rose, and what a semester, what a fall it's been."

Cole heard Bea from the kitchen, "Stay for soup and sandwiches?"

"I can; I'll call mom to let her know I'll hang out with you two; she'll like that."

She looked him up and down, from the top of his head to his toes, "Cole, I swear you've grown."

"I have, Cami, big growth spurt, four inches taller since I saw you in September."

He handed her his jacket and bike helmet. She laid them in a chair in the living room.

"Oh my gosh, and you've gained weight, gosh, you lifting?"

"I am."

"Can tell, you're getting," she stopped, "buffed."

"Uh huh, lifting weights, gonna try for track, or cross country in the spring."

"It was a good soccer season, right?"

"It was," he smiled to her. "But I'm so happy to have a small break; I run as much as I can."

They sat across from each other at the small kitchen island.

"Can we help?" Cole asked Bea.

"Nah, this's so easy, soup and sandwiches. I'll be down in a bit, give you two a chance to talk."

Cami fixed hot chocolate for Cole and her. She put the red rose with its greenery in a vase and set it on the kitchen island for them both to see. They sipped the very hot drink.

"Cami, I've missed you. For a while, after we were together to have the necklace appraised, I thought I might need to tuck you away in my memory. Several ladies at Hillyer wanted to go out with me. So I tried to be with them. But you know what?"

"What?"

She gave him a wide-eyed look.

"They were all about the money, the country club scene, with their parents, talk about their clothes, and hair, and the car daddy would buy them as soon as they turned 16, shallow, materialistic talk. It's a super expensive school we attend, but some kids are absolutely not interested in college, or trying to do something to help out society. They don't even think about what they want to do with their lives when they leave school. Some aimless, some without future goals, just looking for the next party, the booze, and the drug stuff, and they're just sophomores."

Cami touched her shoulder, "Is that any way to live?"

He looked hard into her unflinching green eyes, "It is not my way of living."

Cole saw tears spurting in her eyes, "Cole, after I saw you in September I never heard from a single friend I had at Hillyer. "

"The guy, uh, soccer player?"

"No one, and I thought I'd lost you, too."

"It took a while, but I'm seeing my future, my friendship with you, a lot clearer."

"I told my school counselor, just a few days ago, about my friendship situation at Hillyer, that no one ever got in touch with me again after my parents died and I had to transfer. I told her that I had a disease, that kept them away, the disease of being poor. They dropped me, as if I no longer existed."

"That's right, you no longer existed, but that's in their world."

"Right, I live in a totally different world now. And you know what?"

"What, Cami?"

"My counselor told me that those kids I knew, well, that they weren't really friends."

"That's right, they weren't friends."

"But I still have Justine, and I'm so glad to find out, you, true friends."

They smiled and nodded to each other.

"PSAT?"

"Done, for you?"

"Done."

"How'd you do?"

"I don't test well, and I'm not really that smart," Cole nodded to her.

"Hey, you're smart and you work your butt off."

"I do, how about you?"

"Very well, made the semifinalist list for a National Merit Scholarship," she shook her head, "but with the money mom left me from the insurance, plus the necklace value, well, I'm OK for at least college and maybe a little beyond. So National Merit doesn't matter. I'll have a better chance of getting a HOPE, because of my good grades."

"Yeah, I got a chance for the HOPE. But my folks can afford to help me."

They got up and started the soup and got out the makings for sandwiches.

Cole called his mom. And Bea told him she and Cami would take his bike and him home after it got dark.

The three of them sat together at the kitchen island, eating their soup and sandwiches with gusto. Cami checked with Cole.

"Dessert?"

"What'cha got?"

"Ice cream, cheese cake, berries."

"I choose cheese cake, with berries on top, how's that?"

They cleared the table and brought Bea more coffee.

"Same for me," Bea added.

Cami and Cole fixed three plates of cheese cake with mixed berries on top. They dug in.

"Delicious, and Aunt Bea, I've checked in with Cami, but I'm also concerned about you. You've done some heavy lifting, with your own paralegal work, plus all of the estate duties. How're you?"

Bea raised her eyebrows at his concern for her, "It's been, well," she paused, "very difficult, Cami's been right beside me, most everything's been settled. But I'm certain there're a few surprises ahead in the next months. Cami, you know this, my brother, your dad, he was a difficult person, the richer he became, the more difficult he was. But he cared a great deal for you, his daughter. He couldn't handle it, though, when he lost everything. He and I were in process, of doing pretty much of what actually happened when he and your mom died. It's as if he had some premonition. And Cole, thanks for asking."

Cole put his bike in the back of Bea's pickup.

"Wow," was all Cami could say as they drove to Cole's area. She saw Cole's home, with the beautiful white lights decorating the front of the home and the stately pine trees in the yard.

As soon as they got out of the pickup they hugged. She watched as he got the bike out. They stood together by his garage door and smiled to each other.

"Happy New Year, Cole, and thank you for my beautiful rose."

"Happy New Year to you, Cami, tell your aunt that from me. I know 2008, well it'll be a good year for you, I can feel that. I'm positive, optimistic for you and your aunt. I know we'll see each other again."

Once she got back in the car she asked, "Aunt Bea, would you mind driving next door, to my old place?"

Bea stayed in first gear as they passed the home. New owners put up colored lights, all over the front and on the pines trees in the front yard. Festive wreaths with bright red ribbons adorned the left and right columns on the front porch.

"Wow, they've done such a pretty job of decorating, a warm and cheerful scene. I'm so happy to see this, and I wish the family living there, all the best, from God, and me."

"That's a wonderful thought, the old place, really lovely," added her aunt.

Cami stood in the kitchen when they arrived home. She grabbed the edge of the kitchen counter and let her thoughts spin. She closed her eyes and breathed in deep breaths, in and out.

"I'm almost at the end of this incredible year. Mom and dad, you're beginning to fade from my memory," she whispered

"But still in my heart," she patted her hand over her heart. She held on tight to the handrail ascending the steps to her bedroom.

℅

2008

"That sounds like so much fun, explain please."

"You'll be paid for your time, Cami, and I know your dance and acting abilities. I'm doing it as a volunteer effort, but my helpers, if you decide to, will get a salary. If the effort goes well, we'll do it again in April."

"Thank you, Melinda, I'll check in with my aunt and get back to you."

"Yes, let me know by next Thursday, please."

That night after she did several hours of homework she approached her aunt, who sat at the dining room table, working on a difficult paralegal project.

"Aunt Bea, can we take a break for a few minutes. I got stuff to ask you."

Cami fixed decaf coffee for them, and they moved to the kitchen island.

"Talk to me, my dear," Bea smiled to her niece.

"At the Y the activities director is bringing back an effort that's been gone for several years, but there's been an interest in bringing it back. It's called *A Pirate's Life for Me*. Age is three to six-year-olds with dramatic play, arts, and crafts, and the little kids help us, the older pirate crew, search for hidden treasure. Time is an hour and a half Saturday afternoons, for three weeks in February. Melinda, my dance instructor for many years, is in charge of this project. She called and asked if I'd be interested. It's a volunteer effort on her part, but all of us helpers, we'll get paid a little something for our time."

"I approve, Cami, this is the first time you've asked me about outside activities, which you used to do all the time."

"Yeah, I think it sounds like so much fun, and with each group of little kids it'll be different."

"You'll need a ride?"

"Please, if there are any Saturdays when I can't ride my bike, crummy weather. But I think I'll be OK. Oh, and if the project gets good attendance, the Y plans to offer the pirates play time in late April."

"I can definitely help you with that, Cami."

"Thanks, I'm spending time each day practicing my dancing and gymnastics, and doing some singing and remembering lines from performances I've been in, past years. I want to be ready for the Pirate time. And I'm practicing a lot of my presentations from spirit team at Hillyer. In late March the Ephrine High spirit team sponsor will have tryouts. The team will only be losing four team members to graduation."

ॐ

"What do you think, team? Would you like to try this Pirate effort again, perhaps near the close of school, or during this summer?"

Cami looked at Melinda and saw the nods from the other pirate helpers. She added her own nod.

"I'll take that as a yes from all of you; I'll check into this and let you know as soon as I know."

"It was so much fun, wish I'd done this when I was a little kid," Angela nodded to the rest of the group.

"My favorite part was the play we created each time, the plan for the hunt for the treasure. Each little one had a say as to the physical location of the hunt," Cami added.

"I thought it was such a good idea to stop for healthy snacks, before we did all the physical activities."

Melinda started clapping, "You all did so great."

Soon the whole treasure hunt group clapped and cheered.

"Way to go, Matey."

Melinda gathered them into a big group hug.

Cami rode her bike home that cool but sunny Saturday afternoon. She felt happy, that she accomplished something special, working with the little kids. She mentioned that to her aunt when she got home.

"Aunt Bea, today, wow, today, I did not think about my mom and dad, at all, not until I came down to talk to you."

Her aunt moved to her and gave her a hug.

"Sweetie, you are moving on with your life."

"I am, and I'm so glad."

ॐ

Cami made up her mind. The Ephrine spirit team had open practices, once a week, where visitors could watch the routines the teens learned. Cami showed up that day in early March to watch.

"They're as good as the spirit team at Hillyer. I definitely will try out," she told herself.

She found Justine in the locker room after the practice. They hugged. Several teens watched them as they got ready to leave.

One spirit team member stepped in front of Justine, forcing her to stop.

"Hey, black lady, I'd advise you not to try out for our spirit team. You're good, but you definitely mess up the look of our outstanding group of blondes, redheads and brunettes. You don't fit, do you hear what I'm saying?"

Cami moved away from Justine. Out of the corner of her eye she saw another spirit team member standing nearby.

This teen started to back Justine into a locker. When they got close the teen slammed Justine directly into the locker. Justine's head hit hard against the locker handle.

"Cami, Cami, help me, oh help me."

Justine felt the blood slide down her neck onto her back.

"I'm bleeding."

Cami stood in shock at what she saw, but only for a moment. Her defense skills kicked in. She set down her school bag and moved the teen away from Justine. This girl was strong and started to push Cami back into Justine. But Cami got a grip on the teen and flipped her over onto the tile floor.

Cami started screaming, "Help, someone, please help."

Several team members came running. The girl who observed the whole scene just continued to stand there, her mouth open, in shock. The spirit team sponsor joined them.

Justine sat on the floor in front of the locker. She put her head between her legs. Justine's blood drippled down the locker. The back of her head matted in blood and the back of her green t-shirt was sticky with blood.

"I had to help Justine. I moved the girl away and when she came after me I flipped her."

The girl still lay on the floor, crying softly.

"Call 911, everyone stay right here, until we sort this all out."

When the police arrived, the teens involved gave their statements to the police.   One officer took the girl who attacked Justine away.   The other officers stayed until everyone got picked up by a parent or drove themselves home.   Cami went with Indella and the team sponsor to the ER at Ephrine Memorial. X-rays revealed a slight concussion, and Justine had four stitches to the back of her head.

"Plain and simple," Justine cried as they got ready to leave Emergency, "that girl hated me from day one, did not want a black girl, on that all-white spirit team."

Aunt Bea stood next to Cami as they walked out of the ER with Indella and Justine.

"Ladies, I suspect that girl will not be returning to Ephrine High. And Justine, you need to follow whatever the police tell you that you need to do."

"The girl's parents will get the ER bill. Mom absolutely cannot pay for an expensive visit like that."

"That's very good, Justine, continue to work with whichever officer has your case."

"I want this to be over as soon as possible. I can't believe this's happened to me."

The four women hugged together at Indella's car.

"My headache should go away in a day or so."

"Right, we're praying; God is watching over us."

Justine began to cry again, and Cami held her close, soothing her by rocking her back and forth.

℘

Since after Christmas Bea and Cami attended St. Luke's 8:30 a.m. mass. Always before they attended the 10:30 mass, so now they missed seeing Justine and Cole. Week after week Cami caught a couple out of the corner of her eyes. They sat two rows behind and to the right of where Cami and her aunt always sat for the church service. The first time Cami glanced at them she tried not to stare. Two tall people, a black haired man and his blonde wife stood together.

"Oh dear God, mom and dad, I can't believe it," Cami thought after she turned back to catch a glance at this couple who reminded her so much of her parents. The congregation received communion. They all knelt, until the time when they could sit again. Cami glanced to her right side and back two rows. The couple left, as did a few people after they received communion, not staying for the rest of the mass.

Cami noticed that the man always wore a dark suit, and the woman also wore a dark suit. This continued week after week.

"Aunt Bea, this sounds crazy, but for the past eight Sundays I've noticed an extremely handsome couple at church. They sit two rows back and to the right of us, in the same spot week after week, just like we sit in the same area. After communion I don't see them sitting in the spot where they were earlier. They remind me so much of mom and dad."

Cami touched her aunt's shoulder as they drove from the church.

"Seriously, I'm wondering if I'm losing my mind. Who is this couple? Do I see them in my head, but they're not actually sitting in church? Oh, dear God, do I need to see a shrink?"

"Oh sweetie, please, let me take a look next week. When you see them, whisper to me where they are. I'm glad you've mentioned this to me."

"Well, I felt pretty stupid telling you. But I'm glad I did. It's kinda driving me crazy, me seeing things. Do you think it's my mind, wanting to see my folks so bad, that I'm seeing them in other people?"

"I don't know, Cami, let's just take this one day at a time, OK?"

"Yeah, just like we did and do, every day since my folks died."

"That's right."

ℰℴ

"Mrs. Hampter, you wanted to see me?"

"Yes, Cami, I want you to meet Mrs. Melvini, our drama teacher here at Ephrine."

Cami and the teacher shook hands.

"Please let's sit at my table."

"Your dance instructor over the years, Melinda, suggested I talk with you, Cami."

"She's a wonderful teacher, and in February at the Y I worked with her and little children on a kinda dance, fun kid treasure situation."

"Yes, she told me," Mrs. Melvini smiled to Cami. "Ephrine High's producing the musical, *Brigadoon*. We're just three weeks from production. One of our characters, Maggie, she's come down with mono, and I'm short on understudies."

"I've seen the movie. Wow, isn't this a pretty intense musical for high school?"

"Yes, for sure it is, but we have talent, and willingness from the students involved. Plus we're using the Ephrine Community Auditorium, a much larger stage than the one here at our school."

"Wow, I not sure, but isn't Maggie a dancer in the story?"

Mrs. Melvini nodded to her, "You've a great memory. Yes, she is. She performs a funeral dance for the character, Harry, who fell, and got his skull crushed."

"When Mrs. Hampter told me about your loss," she stopped and paused, "I asked her, well."

Cami paused again.

"Yes, I will try to help you and your musical. I'm getting along with my life since my parents died. And I feel certain I can learn the dance. Maggie, she doesn't have a lot of dialogue, right?"

"That's correct. And Melinda, she assures me, that with your years of dance, that this dance will work for you."

Mrs. Hampter moved away from the two of them. Cami and the director shared the dates and times of the rest of the

practices before the production. Mrs. Melvini gave Cami the
playbook and pointed out the pages involving Maggie's
dialogue and dance.

They left the counseling office together.

"Oh, and Cami, the musical, I think of it as a wonderful
and warm love story. But I hope what everyone can take from
it, the audience, and all my actors, and I'll tell you since
you're just starting with us, that if a person loves deeply
enough, that anything is possible."

Cami repeated, "Love deeply enough, anything is
possible."

"That's right, I'm headed out. Thank you in advance for
helping us, Cami,"

Mrs. Melvini nodded to her, "Save the show."

"I'm getting back to being me, the dancer, the performer,
and I'll practice like crazy on my routine for spirit team
tryouts," she told herself as she got on her bike after that
school day. She smiled almost the whole way home.

ဢ

Cami whispered to her aunt, "They're back there, two rows
back and to the right.

Bea glimpsed over her shoulder. She spotted the couple.
And as Cami described the black-haired man wore a dark
suit, and today the blonde woman wore a light blue suit.

"I do see them, but not up close, and they do not look as if
they fit, because our church goers now dress so much more
casual. I've not seen them before," Bea thought.

She also checked after the congregation received
communion. This time she looked more boldly. She no
longer saw the couple.

Once they got into the red pickup after church Bea turned
to Cami.

"I saw them, Cami. And yes, they were gone after
communion. I'm finding this really creepy. They do seem to

resemble your parents. And I'll keep checking as we continue to attend church. "

"Maybe a vision, from God, for us to have another look at my parents before I put their memories to rest, deep in my heart."

"That certainly could be, God works in really mysterious ways."

ဆ

"*Brigadoon,* it's just a wonderful love story," Cami shared with Justine as they left the school.

"I'm gonna try really hard to have mom come with me to see your perform in the play."

"I hope you both can come."

Cami got on her bike to head to the community auditorium for play practice. Justine rode her bike home. She needed to practice her routine for spirit team tryouts. Every year each spirit team member had to try out for the team. After graduation there would only be three members left on the team. The fourth girl got removed from the school after her involvement with Justine in the locker room. So the sponsor had the remaining team members try out along with eight other girls who expressed an interest in becoming a part of the spirit team.

Justine felt more unsure of herself than ever, because, once again, she was the only black girl to try out. She practiced her routine several times for Cami to observe. And she remembered Cami's bright smile, and encouraging, "You'll have no problem, girl, you been doing this for a year, on the team."

For her tryout Cami combined two different routines she performed as a Hillyer spirit team member. When she finished her routine for Ephrine High's try outs, she wasn't sure how it went. But she liked the enthusiasm the sponsor showed her after she finished her routine. Her day wasn't completed though, because she rode her bike to the civic auditorium for the next to last play practice for *Brigadoon*.

"We've done it, the whole performance, and it went very well," Mrs. Melvini smiled to the entire cast as they assembled on stage. "Tomorrow night brings us to the dress rehearsal, then Thursday, Friday and Saturday evenings we show our community the extraordinary talent you all have."

"Striking the set?" the character Tommy asked.

"Oh, directly after the play; I have volunteer parents bringing pizza and pop as we deconstruct everything and return it all to the storage and costume areas here at the auditorium. It's been wonderful to use this larger stage, especially for the folk dancing."

The cast clapped and cheered their director.

"And we need to especially cheer our sound, music, lighting and set change folks. Having our music on cd means we did not need to involve an orchestra. All these folks worked magic for us."

The cast cheered and hollered for the 10 students who handled all the background work for the production.

80

"I've wanted to talk to you for so long. Has your aunt come yet?"

Aaron looked around for the tall black-haired woman, Aunt Bea.

"She'll be here in about five minutes. Let's sit in the back so we see her when she walks in."

"Tonight's performance, so good, didn't you think so?"

"Yes, everything's synced up really well, our last performance, Saturday night, should be our crowning achievement."

"Aaron, you're superb as Tommy. You and Fiona have such a sensual relationship on stage, the fluid way you dance together, and look at each other. I don't know your background or Stephanie's (uh, Fiona). "

"We've performed together, been in productions at the university, and with a community acting company in town."

"I sure can tell you're so comfortable together."

"When this is over, I want to get to know you, Cami."

"I'd like that. Right now I'm waiting on my results. I tried out for Ephrine's spirit team. I'm hoping I made it. If I did, practices start right away for next year's events."

She paused, "Oh, I see my aunt. Take care, Aaron, with the final performance. We'll talk soon."

"Your funeral dance, for Harry, you're a very talented dancer, how you picked that up so fast, subbing in for the sick girl who played Maggie."

"Thank you, Aaron, see you."

She waved to him as she joined her aunt.

Once they got in Bea's pickup Cami shared, "A boy, actor in the musical, he said he wants to get to know me. He's uber talented, sings, dances, great actor, with a superb voice, both speaking and singing."

"Let me know how it goes with him, Cami."

"I will."

℘

"Thank you, God, for my opportunity to dance, to perform again. I just can't take anything for granted anymore."

Cami thought that as she sat next to her aunt at mass the next morning after the final play performance. She looked for the couple she watched for these last months. They sat there, him in a dark blue suit and her in a pale green suit. For the first time she looked at their faces. Her eyes blurred for a moment. She blinked again and saw her dad and her mom. Hot tears blurred her eyes for a little while. She wiped her nose and looked again, really looking at them. This time their faces were different, a similarity, but not her parents' faces. Her dad looked definitely more Native American, and her mom, more pale than this woman.

After communion Cami knelt, "God, I'm seeing my parents in other people. I guess that's kinda the way it will be, always searching for my folks, even though I know, I just know, they're in my heart, my memory."

She smiled, and she felt a warm glow wrap around her as the congregation sang the last hymn.

"Mom and dad, thanks for being here just now. I just peeked. The couple left after communion, but it's OK; you're with me, thanks for sending the warm glow, uh, you and God."

On the way home Cami shared what happened with Bea.

"Sweetie, maybe after you do some homework, and I get a work project underway, I can talk to you, about the family. I feel pretty sure that your mom never told you much about your dad's and my family history, the Ohay family."

"She did not; I really want to know where I come from, Aunt Bea. And I want to show you something."

80

Cami heard the knock on her door.

"Wanna take a break, come down and chill for a little. I made coffee and there are oatmeal raisin cookies for munching."

"Great idea, I'll be right down."

They sat together, sipping the coffee and having a cookie.

"Aunt Bea, can't believe how good I'm feeling, the old ache is going, the missing them, and I know school's going great. We start spirit team practice, once a week, to learn new routines for next school year."

Cami slid a journal for Bea to see.

"Aunt Bea, years ago dad told me to write, all kinda stuff, what I was feeling, what I dreamed of doing one day. I go back and look at entries I made when I was much younger, fun to read, some of my dreams, my goals, haven't really changed. Uh, the reason to show you this, the message on the front page, from dad. His handwriting, it's sure hard to read, here goes."

"'What is life? Seeing a firefly moving at night; watching the breath of the buffalo in the winter; gazing at a shadow running across the grass and losing itself in the sunset.' Cami, that's from an Indian leader, Crowfoot, of the Blackfoot tribe. In our Canada the Blackfoot are the Siksika."

"Share, Aunt Bea, I'm ready to try to understand what dad said, who your folks are."

"Many Indian sayings have to do with nature. That quote, physical examples of life, that's one way I see life, for me. I'm really glad he shared that with you."

Cami pointed to the word Siksika.

"Yes, that is the name of our Indian tribe."

"I've never heard of it, except in my journal, from dad."

"That's because our Indian family is from Canada, from the province of Alberta."

"Aunt Bea, are you an American?"

"Yes, I am," she paused, "and I see the concern in your eyes. Your dad and I were both born in Georgia. Our parents came to Georgia from a reservation of the Siksika Indians east of Calgary, Alberta. Dad did surveying work and Mom was a kind of nurse, called an LPN. They both got their training in Canada."

"Did they become American citizens?"

"Yes, they did; it's called naturalized."

"So naturalized American citizens."

"That's so they could work and live in the U.S., and they had your dad and me."

"Did they speak their language with you where you grew up in Georgia?"

"Some, I understand a little of the language, and once could speak it just a little, but I've forgotten most everything I knew."

"Mom and dad, they were so young when they had me, so my grandparents weren't that old. What happened; how did they die? My folks never spoke of any of that."

Cami watched her aunt's face change from pleasant to stony, her deep brown eyes clouding as she began to tear up.

"They brought an affliction with them from their reservation. Alcoholism, it reared its head throughout the reservation. Your grandparents started drinking as young teens. They were bright enough to want to learn skills and get away from the reservation. Your granddad had a wonderful opportunity to transfer from a surveying company up north to a division of that company in Georgia. And mom got licensed so she could do her nursing. They had Gilbert, and then three years later, me. When I was 16 and Gilbert 19, just married to your mom, both our parents died, within three months of each other, liver stuff. They took care of us, worked hard by day, sober and hung over, and drunk, always drunk, by midnight."

"Wow, I wondered about something like this, because you handled your brother's death with such understanding, and bravery. Now I know what you saw, growing up, a total destruction of people you loved."

"At the end they drank straight grain alcohol to get the high they craved."

"It musta taken their brains, Aunt Bea."

Bea eyed her niece, "It did, delirium tremens, uncontrollable."

"How horrible."

"Yeah, I drink in a responsible manner."

"Now I know why, oh Aunt Bea, let me hug you."

Cami came around as her aunt stood away from her chair. She held her aunt close as Bea burst into tears. Once she calmed Cami stepped away from her.

"This's been a bad patch for you," Cami looked into her teary dark eyes.

Bea nodded her head and sat back down. She picked up her cup and finished the now cooling coffee.

"I gotta get back to my work, Aunt Bea."

Cami walked away from her aunt. When she got to the stairs, she remembered what she wanted to ask her aunt. She returned to the kitchen island.

"Bea, have you ever thought about Al-Anon?"

"Uh huh, it helped me a lot after my parents died, for about 10 years I was active. I'm good now, really know how to handle sad times, and have gratitude for good times, like having you in my life."

"Good, I'm glad it helped you," Cami nodded and smiled to her aunt.

3

Fall 2009 – Senior Year

"Last week of trail building, how're you liking it by now?"

"Like it, working for the land trust, the exercise, being outside, Aunt Bea, I'm so glad you encouraged me to sign up for it. You're always lookin' out for me."

"It gets you back on the land you kids played on, that you have good memories of."

"Yeah, both Aaron and Cole work on the crew; I guess they didn't want to make great money this summer. They both love the physical labor, just like I do."

"In the olden, really olden days you all might have been farmers."

Cami looked to her aunt as they finished their dinner, "Or have done something in agriculture."

&

Out on the trail Cami observed the guys working ahead of the girls, doing the initial groundbreaking and measuring the width of the trail. She also noticed that Aaron and Cole did not pair up together to do jobs. She decided she might have something to do with that.

During their junior year, Aaron and Cami got the lead roles in the spring play. He kept insisting he wanted to go out with her. But she resisted; she already spent a lot of time with him.

"I'm not getting emotionally close with you, Aaron. Our jobs are acting roles, and that's the way it's gonna stay. I'm scared of intimacy," she shared with him as they began their play practices.

"I'm OK with that; you're missing out, not getting to know the real me," he shared as his eyes bored into hers.

She remembered him saying that. And she thanked him for their keeping a professional distance.

During the trail work she also got to watch a lot of Cole working.

"I love him, always have and always will. He knows, even though I've not said anything to him. He is my special, always friend."

"Cami," she remembered his saying on one of the few dates they had during their junior year, "it's in your caring green eyes, I see your love for me, in your eyes, they're the window right into your soul."

She knew he understood how her senior year would go, spirit team, glee club, and competitions with both groups. She would not have time to participate in school or community plays. His senior year included playing soccer, basketball, and running cross country at Hillyer.

On the final day of trail making each worker brought a lunch plus a special snack to share with everyone else. They sat around in a big circle at a place on the work site where they landed for lunch. Each person placed their snack in the middle for everyone to pick from. Carrots, celery, trail mix, candy bars, popcorn balls, and mixes of nuts got picked up by each person.

"I'm gonna miss this work a lot," Cami whispered as she stood at the beginning trail marker. "So hot, sticky, but really fulfilling, seeing a trail appear like magic, for families to enjoy, from now on."

Cole approached her, "Wanta stick your bike in the back and ride home with me?"

"Hey, thanks, but I want to ride my bike. It's been me and my bike, since mom and dad died. I know, I know, I have a car, which I'll drive to school, but just this last time, I really like the thinking time that I have while I'm riding. And the wind, and sometimes the rain and the cold, in a way I'll miss those things."

"I get it. Whew, did we get in shape doin' this kinda work, or what?"

"Yeah, we did, Cole, but I been tunin' up with spirit team; practices started last weekend."

"Same for me for soccer. I want you to have a great senior year."

"You also," she nodded to him. They came together and hugged.

℘

Ten of them sat around the kitchen island and dining room table. Cami smelled the mix of the tangy beef tacos, the hard corn taco shells, the black beans, and spicy rice as she looked around at the group of hungry girls. They all chowed down.

"This, yeah, this was a really great idea, Aunt Bea," Cami thought as she helped clear.

Ice cream and chocolate chip bars became the next course. The girls lined up to wait their turn for this yummy dessert. The team broke up after that to clean up the kitchen, washing up all the pans and utensils need for the gathering.

Their sponsor, Miss Tristan, spoke to them as they sat around on the floor and living room furniture. It became a back and forth exchange, going over the fall semester of the school year schedule of athletic events in which they would participate. The group agreed that they needed to keep the same uniforms for one more year.

Bea sat in the background, enjoying every second of this get together of young people.

"Really glad I suggested this to Cami, wasn't sure she would fly with it. Like the sponsor says, food always brings folks closer, no matter what age they are. And Cami is becoming more outgoing with this group. She has so much skill, having already been a spirit team member at her other school. Along with glee group, she'll round out her high school years in a super involved way, with young people she really likes, not just with Justine."

For a moment Bea felt wistful, missing all of them, which she would once Cami went away to school. Tears clouded her eyes "And what of me, I need to repurpose my life, and soon, Cami's leaving and she'll just flit back and forth during the rest of my life."

☙

"Sweetie, remember we're doing brunch; it's all prepared, just need to bake the mini-quiches.

Cami nodded to her aunt, "Special occasion?"

"Not sure, hope so."

"Well, tomorrow starts school, so it's a kind of celebration, for me anyway."

"Good, our guest should be arriving in five minutes."

"Mysterious," Cami giggled as she shook her head to her aunt.

When the doorbell rang, Bea spoke out to Cami, "Please get the door, introduce yourself and bring our guest in."

Cami drew herself to her full height of 5'9" and plastered a smile on her face as she answered the door.

"Hello, I'm Cami. Come in, Aunt Bea's waiting for us in the kitchen."

The tall white-haired man stood quite still at the entrance to the front door. He held a small bouquet of yellow, orange, and red flowers in his hand. Cami watched as his other hand went to the side of his face and his eyes widened.

"Yeah, I know, sir, I do that to people, uh, my mom, same face and eyes, but different hair and cheekbones.

"And I, I'm Chet Whetsterfil."

He followed Cami into Aunt Bea's home. Cami introduced them at the kitchen island. She found a vase for the flowers.

"It's good to meet you, Chet; thanks for the flowers. I'll put them at the dining room table. I've got mini-quiches, ready in a few minutes, coffee for you?"

"Yes, black please."

Aunt Bea and Cami sat across from Chet after Cami brought coffee for them.

"Thank you for seeing me, Bea, and Cami," Chet nodded. "I was unbelievably saddened when I heard about the plane crash. How are you doing, Cami, and you also, Bea?"

"It's been two years and a few days; it gets better with the passing of time. Bea is my wonderful guardian; she suffered the loss as I did. And," Cami paused, smiling to her aunt, "I would say that God's blessed us beyond measure. We're grateful."

Bea spoke up, "I concur with Cami."

Cami gazed at Chet for a moment, letting the memories bombard her brain, especially what Cole shared with her.

"I have to tell you, mom's necklace you gave her, it's mine now, safely in my personal safety deposit box. It was suggested that I have it reappraised, so the original appraisal which mom did, plus this new appraisal, uh, all the paperwork, are all kept together with the necklace."

The three of them ate the quiches and mixed fruit and finished off with more coffee. They talked a bit about Chet's horses, especially the one he liked to ride. Cami remembered the name of Priscilla's horse and the one she rode.

"They're all still in the stables and get ridden by my handlers and the folks who come out to ride."

Cami gave Chet a penetrating look and began.

"Mom never told me much about you; she just shared with dad and me that you two rode horses together at the stable you own. Dad seemed glad that mom had that hobby 'cause it seemed to make her happy. She spent a considerable amount of time driving me around to all the activities I participated in after school and weekends. I attended private school, Hillyer, so I had to have a ride to and from school. And she spent time working with her Junior League, PTA, and political activities. So riding was her fun time, and I'm so glad I learned how to ride. I enjoy it," she gave Chet her bright smile.

"After your mom fell from her horse and broke her leg, well, I didn't see much of her after that."

"She had a downward spiral into a pain medication addiction. Her leg never did heal quite right. She planned to go into a facility to help her recover from her addiction. But then, the plane."

Cami shook her head as tears filled her eyes.

"I'm glad you're happy about the necklace. I have no children, so no grandchildren, and my wife's been gone a long time. Now, meeting you, well," he paused and smiled to them, "I really did the correct thing. I was never sure, but now I am."

Cami and Bea cleared the table and brought more coffee.

"There were rumors, all kinds, about the relationship I had with your mom, Cami. It was not, nor had it ever been a sexual relationship. Priscilla was the closest thing I ever had to a daughter. She and I became close; the horses did that for us," he laughed, easing the tension that Cami started to feel about this man.

"She brightened my day, and she felt lonely a lot, your dad, always traveling, always interested in the next big stock win. To be rich, and rich in a hurry, like your folks were, difficult. People projected jealousy toward your parents, resentment. I never felt they got treated properly at the country club, where they became members early in your dad's career. People looked down their noses at new money," he paused, "terrible."

"Thank you, Chet, for sharing all of this with me. I'm so happy that you got to have a daughter, to share what it's like, the ups and downs of young womanhood. Mom was 17 when she had me; gosh she's still a young person, so you got to know what it's like to hear about a granddaughter."

"Your mom loved you so much, Cami."

"I sure know that."

"With your Aunt Bea here, I'd like to request that I might see the two of you from time to time. I know your folks died very young."

Bea nodded her head, "We're pretty much without family, Chet. What do you think, Cami?"

"That would be really wonderful, to get to know Chet better."

She looked at her aunt.

"Do you ride, Aunt Bea?"

"I do, but not for a long time."

"Well, we'll have to try to get together," Cami noted, "when you're here in Ephrine."

"I live in northern California, part of the year. But I always come here in the summer, I don't mind the heat and humidity, my horses bring me back."

"What're your interests in northern California?"

"Wineries, I watch over several, uh, I should say, folks help me watch over ones I own."

Cami smiled to him, "Wow, you've got a super lot going on in your life."

"It keeps my mind active, but my favorite thing, the horses, and riding for as long as I can, the wind across my face, that freedom I feel."

They sat together in silence for a little time.

"After high school, what for you, Cami?"

"Applying to Georgia Tech, stay in state. I'm also trying for the HOPE scholarship, to help me."

"Tell me about HOPE."

"For all students in Georgia, based on high school GPA, test scores, and other high school/outside activities, for students who plan to stay in Georgia for their collegiate careers. It pays for tuition; grades have to be kept at a certain level, below that, the scholarship's gone. The state's just trying to keep students doing their best, graduating from college."

"That's quite a commitment from the state."

"It is; I'm headed for engineering, probably civil, bridges, water, that kind of situation. I super groove on my science and math courses; I have classes at both Ephrine High and Humphrey University, the math, econ, and government at Humphrey. So I'm already in college credit stuff."

"Come on, Cami, share the rest," her aunt urged her.

"Oh, I'm on the spirit team, a school spirit group, like cheerleaders, except we dance, do gymnastics moves to music, and we celebrate other great stuff that happens at Ephrine, like when our band wins state awards, or when cross country wins a meet, that kind of stuff. I'm also in the school glee club, a boy/girl singing and dance group."

"Your mom used to share about your dance, and gymnastics training."

"Yeah, I had lots of years with those groups and many others, thanks to mom."

"And you, Bea?"

"Econ grad, Georgia Southern, then paralegal training course at a university in Atlanta, have gotten my accreditation. More and more, I'm handling real lawyer-like stuff at the law office where I've worked for the past few years here."

"Like it?"

Bea smiled to Chet, "Very much, so challenging."

Cami touched her aunt's shoulder, "She brings home work, sometimes quite a few hours."

"Uh huh, lots of law stuff is research, the work downright labor intensive."

"You both have very full lives."

Both Cami and Bea nodded to him.

"Cami's parents' estate's settled, all the little things took time, but we're certainly moving on with our lives."

"From tragedy to blossoming lives, for both of you."

"Thank you, Chet."

"Would you mind walking me out, Cami?"

"Of course."

They stopped, almost to the end of the sidewalk in front of Bea's home.

He turned and faced her.

"You're taller, but those eyes, Cami, you truly are your mom."

She smiled and nodded to him.

"Wanted to ask you, do you know if your aunt has a special guy?"

Cami shook her head, "No she does not, and that surprises me a little. What she's done since my folks died is take care of me, but I'll be gone away to school soon. She works so much; I am so glad I can drive, and have a car to drive to school and university. Do you know someone for my aunt?"

"Yes, my foreman at the stables; his first marriage failed, no kids, he's lonely, but sure isn't finding anyone around here."

"Wanta play matchmaker?"

"I could."

"You need to know, if you can't tell by looking at my aunt."

"Oh yes, she sure looks completely native American."

"She tries, always to be very professional looking keeps her hair shoulder length and curled, eye makeup to bring out her deep inset dark brown eyes."

"What tribe?"

"Siksika."

"Wow, not familiar."

"Uh, my grandparents on dad's side were Canadian, from an Indian reservation outside of Calgary, Alberta. They became naturalized American citizens after they moved to Georgia. So Bea and Gilbert, my dad, were born in Georgia."

"You do not look native. But you do have that beautiful tan, and a bit of the cheekbones."

"Pretty much my mom," tears began in Cami's eyes, "I, I'm grateful I've had this opportunity to meet you. My mom's whole situation, her last few years, bothered me so much."

Chet watched as a small smile began on Cami's face. It grew until she beamed into his eyes.

"May I hug you?"

"Course, Chet."

She felt his tall frame and arms enclose her in a gentle hug. She stepped back and waved to him as he started to drive off. Cami stood in the early afternoon sunlight, feeling a warm glow surround her.

"Thank you, God, for your grace directed to me. I must always be positive about what's happening in my life. I really thought the ugliest and worst of that relationship between mom and Chet."

&)

Every day of the week Cami drove to Humphrey University from 10:30 to 1:30, for her alternating integral calc and the microeconomics classes. Then she hurried back to Ephrine High for Glee Club three days a week in the afternoon. The other two days she studied in the school library. After school, on Tuesdays and Thursday she had spirit practice until 4:30.

"Go rest for a half hour," Cami told herself.

She did, in her room, then got up and started dinner or checked on how the crockpot dinner cooked up. She continued on her homework, then dinner, then more homework. Two nights a week, she took a break from the work, and cleaned bathrooms, her own, and the half bath on the first floor on one night, vacuumed the home the other night. Bea and Cami did their own wash, towels and sheets. By the week before Thanksgiving she caught a cold.

"I'm doing too much; glad I'm not singing in glee, until my voice recovers."

On the Thursday morning before the week off for the Thanksgiving holiday, Cami took her temp, 101, and her right ear ached. Bea took her to her own doctor's office where a nurse practitioner looked her over.

"Stay home from school tomorrow; this antibiotic's powerful, and you need to rest. Do you have a lot going on for the coming holidays?"

Cami explained her glee, spirit and ball she planned to attend.

"Only participate if you're feeling much better. This's affected not only your ear but also your voice, caution," she shook her head to Cami. "You don't want to lose your singing voice," the nurse practitioner warned her.

Bea took her home. Cami lay down on the couch and waited for her aunt to bring the medication home. Bea woke her so she could take the pill. She helped Cami walk upstairs to her own bedroom. The ear problem made her balance out of whack. Bea went to work but came home earlier than usual.

"Sweetie, you need to eat this soup and crackers. You have so little in your tummy, the antibiotic can upset you."

Bea sat with her as Cami perched on the edge of her bed, taking small spoonfuls of her favorite soup, tomato.

"That does taste good. But I'm ready to go back to bed. Could you please call Justine, have her get my homework from Ephrine? I'll have to deal with my classes at Humphrey on my own. If I'm feeling up to it tomorrow, I'll e-mail my profs, let them know. Oh my goodness, I'm so glad I don't have any exams at either school, tomorrow, before our week off."

"I'll take care of Justine, call her. I'll have to go in early tomorrow, and I have about four hours of work, before bed for me."

"Thanks for all you do for me, Aunt Bea."

"You're my family, young lady."

"Go, I don't want you getting sick from my awful germs."

Cami slept from 7 p.m. that night until Bea woke her the next morning as she was leaving.

"I called school that you were sick. You've all next week to get better."

Cami waved her hands as she whispered from her bed, "Voice, gone."

"My gosh, whatever it is, it's spread, like the np said, ear, better?"

Cami nodded. She started crying, harder and harder.

"I'm so sorry you're sad, sweetie, you take it easy today, and I'll call you at noon."

Cami held out her arms and Bea came to hug her. Bea watched her tear-stained face as she scooted back under the covers and closed her eyes. That seemed to calm her.

"God, help me with Cami," Bea spoke out as she headed for work. Tears blinded her eyes for a moment, "I can't lose the young person I love so much."

Before Bea took her lunch break, she called home.

"Cami, how're you feeling?"

She heard her niece crying. Bea let her cry for a little.

"Did your voice come back?"

Cami sobbed, then in strangled whispers to Bea, "Gone, voice gone, sad, sad Aunt Bea."

She began crying again.

"I'll come home soon, sweetie. Go down and have something to eat. All you've had are water and your antibiotics so far today. They may be affecting you somehow."

Bea checked with several staff at her office. She explained that Cami had not really been sick, not on antibiotics except a couple of times earlier in her life that she could remember. They advised Bea to watch Cami, especially about the crying, her sadness.

When she got home that afternoon she saw Cami sitting at the kitchen island, her books spread out around her.

Bea hugged Cami and noticed that she dressed in her Ephrine sweatshirt and blue jeans and brushed her hair into a ponytail. She read Cami's note.

Justine came, brought my school work. I e-mailed my profs and got what I need. My voice gone, throat aches, ear feels better. Antibiotic, think it's making me sick. I can barely keep toast down. And I'm having horrible dreams when I rest, black nightmare figures shrieking, and flying all around me.

Cami worked for a few minutes longer, then gathered her books and papers and went up to her bedroom. A while later Bea heard banging against a door. She rushed up the stairs and found Cami on the bathroom floor. Bea smelled the vomit from the stool.

"Was that your last medicine and food?"

Cami nodded her head as Bea helped her to her bedroom.

"So weak, think it's the antibiotic, think I'm allergic or something," Cami wrote out.

"Try to rest, Cami, tomorrow morning, we're going to Urgent Care."

Cami nodded to Bea, then closed her eyes. Bea covered her with a blanket, not wanting to disturb her sleep. Cami woke and sat bolt upright about 2 a.m. She tried to speak but could not. Even the whisper was worse. She turned on the lamp at her bed table, grabbed the notepad she used to communicate with Bea and started a new sheet of paper. She wrote as fast as she could, trying to get out the words as she got rid of everything in her stomach earlier.

"I've lost everything in my life

Mom and Dad are dead, now over two years

My beautiful home, gone, all the wonderful furnishing, sold, everything

Our property, my special play area I had with my friends, no more and no more walks, back into the pine trees on our land

I attended a great school, special and private. I took so many grand classes, dance, sing, perform, voice, gymnastics, karate, painting, horseback riding, and even woodcarving – lots of other stuff

I miss my spirit team at Hillyer and all the good we did, the school spirit we helped raise up

I can't hear very good in my ear that had the infection and I don't know if or when I'll get my voice back

The nightmares awful and I've just started having them since I got sick

഻

"Cami, so glad you were able to rest, I'm Dr. North. Do you remember your aunt bringing you in to Urgent Care?"

Cami shook her head. She felt a hand touch her hand not connected to the IV drip and turned to see her aunt.

"Sweetie, we've been here for a few hours," Bea smiled to her.

"Yes, Cami, we're rehydrating you. Your aunt's given us your situation. You're on a totally different antibiotic. We've decided you are definitely allergic to penicillin. I've also read this page you wrote out in the night, plus your nightmares you're having. Your mind's kinda whacked right now."

Cami nodded her head, and she smiled a tiny smile for the doctor. She whispered to go to the bathroom and when she returned the doctor had gone.

"We'll go home, when they check you over in a half hour. You won't be taking any more antibiotic by mouth. What you've taken by IV should take care of your ear. The doc says it looks better, it's draining. And you've got to drink plenty of liquids, especially at home. You're getting some crackers and a pop to help you burp. That'll be the test, if you can keep that down we'll go home. The doctor thinks maybe for you to spend some time with Cole, to go over the paper you wrote. I told her about your long-time friendship with him. Justine, just not right to have her hear all this. You're such a positive, optimistic person."

Cami wrote out on the pad, *"Not now, bad patch, remember when the folks first died I thought I had got all this, understood. Well, I don't got this. There're so many regrets right now, the sadness back."*

Cami began to cry and rock side to side, then wrote, *"I'm so sorry, Aunt Bea, I'm sick, and I want to just get away from everything."*

Bea nodded to her, "Cami, back to just one day at a time, we gotta get you feeling better and out of the funk you're feeling."

Within an hour Bea helped Cami into their home. Cami started to cry and held out her arms to Bea. They held each other close and Bea heard her strangled whisper, "Thank you."

That evening Bea fixed tomato soup and toasted cheese sandwiches for them as they ate in front of the toasty fire.

"Uuummm," Bea heard Cami's sound.

At Bea's urging Cami had a small portion of warm apple crisp. She started to feel weary. On her notepad she wrote, *"I'm going to watch mass on TV in the morning. I miss going to church. God's not been talking to me. Except for you I feel alone in the world. Can't believe how much I miss mom and dad, like I did after they died."*

When Cami came up the steps to her room she noticed clean pj's laid out on her bed. And her aunt washed her sheets and pillowcases.

"I'll shower; I don't honestly know when was the last time I got clean, oh Aunt Bea, so gross, thanks for washing my stuff."

Bea watched as Cami gave her a small smile. After her shower and washing and drying her hair, Cami lay in bed, smelling all the fresh washed bedding. She wrote on her note pad.

"I think I'm feeling better. Aunt Bea says Cole will visit."

She showed her writing to her aunt.

Bea hugged her and then placed Cami's *Bible* next to her.

"This book brings me such comfort, maybe it will you," she looked into Cami's tired eyes.

Her niece nodded, scooted into bed, and closed her eyes. Her aunt turned off her bedlamp but left the door ajar. Cami had a whistle, in case she needed Bea. When she stepped outside Cami's room she walked several steps, leaned against the wall and slid down in a heap. Bea felt hot tears fill her eyes.

She whispered, "Dear God, please help Cami and me. We need you, please be beside us."

Cami woke up early the next morning, wrapped herself in her warm robe and settled on the couch in the family room to watch mass. She brewed a pot of coffee and fixed toast with jelly for herself.

Bea joined her for the last few minutes of the mass.

"Your voice, sweetie?"

Cami looked at her aunt and shook her head.

"Time, it'll take time," she patted her niece's hand.

ℂ

"Oh my gosh," Cole whispered to her after they hugged, "you've lost weight; you really've been sick."

Cole stepped back and looked into Cami's solemn green eyes, no light shining from them this day.

They sat next to each other at the kitchen island. Bea left earlier to buy groceries and give them time together. Cole read through the words she wrote when she felt the grimmest she'd ever felt in her life. He looked the paper over a second time and then pressed his hand over the page.

"I know you can't talk, too much strain on your vocal cords, I got that."

Cami nodded to him.

"Are you starting to feel any better?"

She wrote, "*Uh huh, watched mass this morning, am able to eat, starting to taste good.*"

"You're not trying to exercise, right?"

"*Right, too weak right now; if we could I'd like to go for a walk for a few minutes. I miss being outside so much.*"

"So, gotta go in a few minutes, soccer's good, we may make quarterfinals; my classes, so hard, take so much time, homework, but I'm tryin' to stay healthy."

Cami nodded to him.

"Your homework?"

She gave him a thumbs up.

"Thanksgiving?"

"Not sure, depends on how I feel; been invited to friends."

"I asked you a while back, I would like you to go to Hillyer's Holiday Ball with me. You agreed. But now I don't know."

She nodded to him.

"So as we've talked about before, Cami, one day at a time, again, back to that. God's planning for us; we gotta trust in him, let stuff unfold as He wants it to, not how we want things to go. That's so hard. That's enough, 'cause you're so down right now. All of us, uh, take steps forward, and then steps back in our time here on Earth. Your life is so important, so many are counting on you, glee, spirit, your profs at Humphrey. You're a shining star there, doing that university work and doing it well."

"Thanks, it'd help me a lot if you would call me once during our break through Thanksgiving. I need to try to look forward to Christmas, semester end at both schools, and I really want to go to Hillyer's Holiday Ball with you. I gotta get better 'cause I don't have a dress for the ball, shopping."

"I'm no girl, but I think you should consider shopping for a dress you can also wear for Prom, if you decide to go your senior year. Oh, and the dress oughta be one to work for dances and stuff at your college."

Cami nodded to him.

"I'm seeing your eyes; you're getting more weary by the minute. No walk today, I want you to go rest; I'll call you, better yet, let's e-mail plus a call, me talkin'," Cole smiled to her as they stood and hugged.

"Cami, God loves you, and so do I."

She saw him out and grabbed the handrail, hauling herself up to her room. She slept until Bea called her for dinner.

℥

"Happy Thanksgiving, Bea and Cami. Meet Jake Sheaman, he runs the place," Chet smiled to the women and then to his foreman. Bea and Cami shook hands with Jake. Cami felt Jake's rough, calloused hand in his strong handshake.

"Cami, are you getting your voice back?" Chet asked.

Bea answered for her, "A little, but any talking's a strain, so she's a pretty quiet kid right now." Bea paused, "She's getting good at writing her thoughts out."

Cami nodded to her aunt and smiled to the men.

"You're almost a twin, Cami," Jake commented, "Priscilla, except for your hair color."

Cami pointed to her eyes.

Jake nodded, "Yup, they're a match."

Everyone giggled, lightening the mood.

"We'll eat, my cook says, in five minutes. We'd like to show Bea around the stables after."

"Sounds great, Chet," Bea nodded.

Cami raised her hand.

"My goodness, you can come also; Jake's got a lot to show you both."

℥

Cami marveled at how good the smoked ham, tiny red potatoes, salad, and rolls tasted.

She wrote on her pad, "*YUM!*" and showed it to Chet.

"I'll let cook know."

"Save pumpkin pie for after our tour?"

The women agreed.

After the meal Bea stayed with the men, getting lots of her questions answered. Cami wandered around the stable area, letting memories pepper her brain. She walked to the running track. She could see her smiling mom, with her blonde hair streaming behind the helmet she was required to wear. Cami watched the vision ahead move around the track. Then she turned from the track, tears welling up in her eyes.

"Mom, the helmet saved your head, but you still broke your leg in the fall. That was the beginning of the end for you," she thought.

Her mind whirled through memories of the last times with her folks, and then the two years now with Aunt Bea.

"God, help me, bring my voice back. I gotta move forward with my life, with being grateful, and trying to be happy with what You've given me."

She found the three of them on the other side of the stables.

"Did you see your horse, Cami?"

Cami nodded to her aunt.

"Maybe we could come riding one day."

Cami nodded again and smiled to the three of them. She observed her aunt and Jake as they walked ahead of Cami and Chet.

"She stands eyeball to eyeball with him. I like him, don't know what happened, to his marriage. Gosh, stuff like that is sure beyond me. We'll see, maybe a match?" she questioned.

They had coffee, pumpkin pie and whipped cream, sitting in front of the warm fire in the great room.

"I'll be taking off after the New Year, back to see how the wine's doing. Bea, check your calendar, I'd like to invite you, Cami, and Jake to be my guests at the Club for New Year's Eve. I haven't gone," he paused and looked up with a strangled "since I lost her."

Bea looked at Cami, "Let's see how our little gal's doing, and I'll check my calendar, and get back to you."

"Fine," Chet nodded.

൭

"We want to share the holiday spirit with all of you. Please join in as we move among you and sing our Christmas carols."

The glee singers, dressed in red or green and wearing reindeer headgear or holiday bows moved among the elderly folks gathered in the large room at their senior facility. Cami watched the smiles on the faces of many of the seniors as they sang along with the young people.

"What a great idea this was, including the folks in the singing, not just singing to them, but having them join in with us. Thank you God for giving me back my voice, even if I'm an alto now, and no longer a soprano," Cami thought as she moved among the seniors with the rest of her glee singers.

Her group did not leave after the singing. They stayed, siting at tables with the seniors, bringing them drinks and cookies for all of them to share. They spent a half hour chatting about old Christmas days with the folks. Then it was time for them to depart. The senior care person in charge suggested that the singers might want to come back the next year. Cheers went around among the seniors. They really liked the young people, their singing and enthusiasm. As the glee group gathered together they sang "We Wish You a Merry Christmas" to the seniors. That met with more applause and cheers. Hugs went all around between the two groups.

Cami walked with several glee members out of the facility.

"As they are, so we will become," one teen said as they got to the parking lot.

The girls nodded to each other.

"It was so fun; what fine folks they are," Cami spoke out.

"Agree," the other girls smiled as they said their goodbyes.

Cami drove home, a warm glow flowing over her, "Doing for others, I like that so much."

୫୦

Cole looked up the stairs as Cami came down slow, holding the railing. He noticed she wore low heels, as he saw her do for mass.

"The deep rose color of her beautiful dress, it brings out the green of her gorgeous eyes, she's," he gulped, "perfect."

"My, oh my," he whispered as he hugged her.

"Thanks, my first big girl real party dress," she smiled to him.

Bea stood, watching them from the kitchen.

"Wow, there're so young," she paused, thinking back to the times she saw them together, "first love?"

And then Bea remembered how Justine, Cole, and Cami approached her as she had to tell them of the parents' deaths two years before. Cole stood between the two girls. They held on tight to each other, friends.

"Still a wonderful friend for Cami," she whispered and nodded.

୫୦

"You're so light in my arms, can tell you're a dancer, like your feet seem to barely touch the floor."

"Been doin' the dancing most of my life. But Cole," she raised her eyes up to his, "it's wonderful the way you hold me, your strong lead, dancing with a partner, oh wow."

"Same for me, I'm having such a good time with you. I can't believe you'll be leaving me, like soon."

"Cole, we'll see each other during breaks from university. And, we are going to meet lots of other people, at school. How do we know what we really want until we experience life with different people?"

"You're right, I'm just getting a little anxious about school, not as confident as you are, Cami."

"Hey, we gotta enjoy this, your big dance at your school. And I'll do Prom at Ephrine. Let's go sit down please. I still don't have all my energy back from being sick."

They sat at a table with other much younger Hillyer students. Everyone got invited to the Ball. As in previous years as a student Cami always felt a surprise at the number of elementary and middle school students who came. Cami and Cole complimented the younger students on their nice outfits, the boys decked out in suits or tuxedoes and the girls in pretty party dresses.

Cole noticed the look in Cami's eyes as they returned to the dance floor.

"I saw your eyes, Cami, as we got up. You gazed around at all the beautiful young people at this amazing school."

"Tell me."

"You all have so much, is what I saw your eyes say to this group. And what I think your mind said was that all of this can be taken away in an instant. All of us, students at Hillyer, come from some kind of money or scholarship, or we wouldn't be getting this very expensive and special education."

He held her close.

During the next slow song, she spoke, "Appreciate what you have, please. I certainly did not. But now, now I am forever grateful for what I have in my real life."

"Yes, be grateful, I try to thank God as often as I can for all He's bestowed on me and my family."

They heard a fast song begin. Cami liked swing dancing.

As they began she touched his shoulder and gave him her wide smile, "Fly with me."

He nodded to her and smiled, and they did.

ॐ

Finals and Christmas slipped away. Cami sat with Jake on one side of her and Chet on the other side. Bea sat across from Cami. She heard the music from the small orchestra playing in one corner of the biggest room in the country club.

She remembered helping her mom decorate for this New Year's Eve Party one year. The decorations this year seemed subdued, lots of silver and gold net, silver and gold balloons. That year she helped her mom; red was the decorating color. Bright and cheerful, her mom told her the next day after the party. Cami did not go to the event that year, but stayed behind, inviting Justine to spend the night.

Chet asked Cami to dance once dessert was cleared.

"You're as light, like a tiny bird, all those years of dance."

"All this is so easy for me. And I want to tell you how much I appreciate the invitation. I've never attended. For a few years mom and dad always came. Then they stopped, I guess I kinda know why."

"That's right, Cami, new rich, lots of conflicts."

Cole spotted her on the dance floor with an older gentleman. He got a sick feeling in his tummy.

"I wonder if that's the horseman?"

He stood and looked to the table where Aunt Bea sat with another man.

Cole's mom saw the somber look on her son's face as he stood. She touched his arm, "Honey, go talk to Cami, you could invite her to dance."

He looked down at his mom, "Sure surprised as heck to see her here."

"Have the guts, have the guts," he kept telling himself as he approached the table where Cami sat with her aunt and the gentlemen.

After Cami made introductions, she got up and danced with Cole.

"Almost 2009, oh Cami, it's a shock to see you here."

"Yeah, that's the horseman, mom's friend. I couldn't tell you what was going on because I lost my voice."

"Feel like sharing?"

"Uh huh," she spoke in a soft voice, "mom and Chet had a kind of daughter and father relationship. There was never sex, but a love of horses and being outside together. Dad wasn't home, and Chet lost his wife some time ago. It turned out to be a nice relationship for my mom. And I learned to ride, even had a special horse out at the stables, whew," she paused, "so much better than I'd expected, relieved beyond belief."

Cole held her closer as they danced.

"I'm so glad you told me; sounds like it was a special relationship."

"Chet said it was, and mom, I sure could tell, seemed happier after she'd been riding, like it brought her a special peace, kinda like for me being outside, riding my bike, hiking, stuff like being in motion, that does it for me."

"And for me too, outdoors is calming."

"Yeah, even when you're doing sports."

"Right."

"Can you come to my table for a minute, I know my mom and dad would like to see you again."

After the dance Cole led Cami to his table. His dad stood up and shook hands with Cami as did Cole's mom.

"So grown up, and those eyes, positively to die for, as were her mom's eyes," Cole's dad remembered.

The family asked how she was and she shared a couple of stories from the past two years. Cole and Cami excused themselves to dance a fast swing dance.

When they finished dancing, Cami held his hand and looked into his eyes,

"We flew again," she emphasized, "again."

Cole nodded and smiled to her, "Can I come by your table about midnight?"

"'Course, we'll see this new year in."

They smiled, looking into each other's eyes, "Together."

ℰℭ

"This'll be special, Justine."

"Yeah, Cami, can't believe Cole invited me, he said it was a New Year's resolution, to try to see us more."

Cami raised her arm and waved to him as he stood near the entrance of the restaurant. He spoke to the host who ushered him to their table.

"Guys, so sorry, I got jammed up with a cross country run that took too long."

"We're just glad you're able to be here."

Justine shook her head to him, "Since of course, you invited us. This is a pretty special place, glad you suggested the proper attire. And we'd like to thank you now, for inviting us, for spending time with us. "

"Well, mom felt I needed to do this with my special forever pals. It's gonna be a super busy semester, and I don't know when I'll see you ladies again, our different schools. I'm so glad I got to see you two as part of Ephrine's spirit team in November."

"Oh yeah, when we showed up at the soccer game between our two schools."

"Your routine, ladies, was completely awesome, such gymnastics and dance moves. Our spirit team at Hillyer performed at a football game that night."

The three of them ate hearty, and when dessert arrived with coffee they lowered their voices. They looked around and saw that their placement at a table in a corner of the restaurant would be perfect for their conversation.

"So what's it like to be a hormone-driven almost 18-year-old male, at a school like Hillyer, where everyone is in uniform."

Cole looked cross-eyed at his two friends.

"What the h--- do ya think. Remember ladies,"

"Uh huh, yeah, we know, you've told us for the past few years, you sometimes have a sexual thought nearly every minute, so 60 thoughts an hour," Cami nodded to him, a bemused look on her face.

Cole watched her eyes, bright green, shining, laughing to his eyes. He looked at Justine. She directed that same look toward him.

"It's an absolute bitch to be around some girls at school. It's a good thing they're in uniform. But I have the vision of what's beneath. Ladies, it's terrible to be a guy."

"That's why you love runnin', being in sports."

"Uh huh, sure takes the edge off the horniness that's pretty constant in my life."

Cami and Justine began to giggle. It was infectious and soon Cole joined in.

Before it got loud Cami touched Justine's shoulder and then Cole's.

It sobered them for a bit.

"And ladies, is it harder for you, now that your sexuality's beginning to really be a part of you?"

"Much harder, guys seem much more attractive, more conflicted, not just like the goo-goo-eyed, pawing 9th and 10th graders."

"I agree with Justine. But, I'll say it, 'cause I'm interested in love and sharing, that a guy's not just gonna own my vagina."

Cole opened his eyes wide when his brain understood what she just said to him.

"You ladies are generous and kind, hope-driven women, not pieces of property on a guy's arm."

"Amen," Justine and Cami said together.

℘

She only met them once before. Cami shook her head at what she did, driving herself to her grandparents' home, to help out with construction during spring break. They asked her to meet them at the church worksite.

Cami looked up at the pale blue sky, looking for rain clouds after she got out of her car.

"Whew, maybe not today," she whispered as she gathered her gear from her trunk, her tool belt, steel-toed boots, and a cap with a Georgia Tech patch. She found her way to the new construction, a hall next door to the small church.

"It's further along than I anticipated; dry wall's done and primer paint."

Cami touched a spot on the side of the room.

"Dry," she noted.

She wandered down the hall noticing a stage that took up the whole far side of the room. A small kitchen, complete with appliances and cabinets, found a home in a small section of the left side of the room.

"Cami, you're here," she heard a man's voice as he came to her.

She put down her gear and looked up to the tall man with the ball cap on. For a moment she was not sure who he was, his hat.

"Yes, I know, hard to recognize me, my beard and hat, it's Granddad Jacob, how was your trip?"

She nodded to him, "Hi Granddad, my trip good, beautiful weather, an easy drive."

"Your grandma will be here in a few minutes. She and a helper are bringing the paint for the walls on this level. I have a crew in the basement. They've put on the primer paint over the dry wall. I have your drawing of the bookcase you want to help build down there. Your timing's excellent, after you've built it with a helper, then we'll put it up against the painted wall."

"It can be moved from location to location; the wood I'm using will not be that heavy."

"I've put all the wood, nails and saws you'll need in a corner down there, you'll need room to work."

"Paint, or stain, or varnish on the bookcase, after we've built it?

"Just varnish, I want to get it up, because we have all the shelves designated with items we want to put down there."

"When that's done, I can help with the change you want at the church entrance."

"That's right, we'll need lots of helpers to get that task done."

"Cami," she heard from the entrance to the basement.

Cami turned, to see her grandma walk toward her. They hugged.

"I'm so glad you're here; thank you for helping out. It means a lot to us," Grandma Jess whispered to her.

℘

Cami stood in line as the Friday evening potluck began. Otis stood next to her.

"I'm so glad I got a chance to get to know you this week, Cami, to be your helper. You got so many skills, where'd you learn to do construction stuff?"

"Classes at school, woodworking, beginning construction, mom always had me in classes at community college, at the Y, dance, acting, and stuff like this. It's what I'm gonna do after university.

"What's that?"

"Civil engineering, so bridges, buildings, maybe stuff with water."

They took their loaded plates and sat in the grass next to Cami's grandparents. They sat in picnic chairs. Everyone else sat around in a big half circle, some on the ground and some in chairs.

Cami listened to the sounds of the conversations, some laughing, but everyone seemed tired and happy. She felt the contentment in the faces of the group. She worked long hours that week, as did many of the rest of this group.

"I hope everybody's efforts will really bring this church together, Otis."

He turned and smiled to Cami between bites.

"It'll help, sure seems like we have new members of the church. I know my folks are pleased, to have the church spruced up, and the adjoining hall being built. Did you know we had an anonymous donor pay for the church hall?"

"Yeah, my grandparents told me; they've been busy folks since they got here, to grow the church membership and to fix the church up."

"Well, they're doing that, for sure. Cami, I finally heard that your folks were killed in a plane crash a couple years back. I'm so sorry. You seem happy and wanting to help folks. How'd you do that?"

Cami's green eyes pierced his brown ones, "God, we're in His hands. I had an awful time with being patient, while He decided how to help me go on living. And my Aunt Bea took me in. She's my dad's sister. And she is," Cami stopped talking and nodded, "an angel, sent straight from God."

"Oh my goodness, an angel, yeah. And I forget, it's His will for us."

"Yup, I'm in two classes at the university in my town, uh, getting college credits. That's me moving on. When I finish high school, I'll almost be a sophomore at Georgia Tech."

"So you'll start in the fall?"

"Uh huh, living in a dorm on campus."

"You?"

"Gotta start at a community college; my grades, mediocre, and I'll not get much help from my folks. You got a HOPE, right?"

"I did, and I intend to make grades every semester, to keep the scholarship through my entire time at Tech."

"What about this summer?"

"Sweet, oh my gosh," she smiled to him, "I got so lucky, gonna work with Lormer Construction in Ephrine. They're doing bridge work in several locations on country roads outside of town."

"But you'll still live with your aunt?"

"Uh, huh, she's my family."

"Maybe I could drive down and see you sometime this summer."

"Yeah, nice, that would be nice; I'd want to show you construction work, on a bridge, my world."

Once everyone settled in with their desserts, Jacob Standin spoke.

"Thank you, one and all, for everything you've done this week; weather held so we could do the work at the church entrance. Our granddaughter, Camilla Ann Ohay, or Cami," he stopped and smiled to her, "joined in this effort. She's going into engineering in college, wanted to help us, so she drove here from Ephrine on her spring break. It just happened to coincide with our work session. She designed and built, with help from Otis, the shelving in the hall basement. So many of you've done so much in so many regards. My church supervisor thanks you also. It's kinda a miracle, don't ya think?"

Everyone set their plates down and clapped and cheered for the effort made for their own congregation.

℘

Cami drove home. As she neared Ephrine, she spoke out loud, "Dad and mom, I know you're proud of me for helping out your folks, mom. I know I helped mend some old broken-down fences. I really enjoyed what I was doing, and Granddad Jacob and Grandma Jess, well they thanked me."

"Whew," Cami blew out a breath as she brought in her bags from her church adventures. She spoke out, "I just gotta keep growing, in my faith, in my helping folks out, caring for those around me. And I've met a nice guy at my grandparents' church, very different from Cole or anyone I've gotten to be around. He's closer to God than anyone I've known; he seems like one of the followers of Jesus from the olden days."

ℰꙨ

Cami watched her Glee Club members as they danced and sang on the Ephrine High stage, preparing for the multistate glee competition.

"We'll do well, may not take first, but we'll be close."

"Music of My Heart" was the song the group performed for the competition at Auburn, Alabama. And Cami thought right, they came in second, but the group seemed happy.

"There's always next year," their teacher shared as they made the long drive back to Ephrine.

"But not for all of us," one of the seniors chirped out. The group laughed.

The sponsor's retort came quick, "So for you, not returning to us, there are competitions at the university level. I certainly hope, if you can, at least continue to sing, or to dance, somehow, somewhere."

And then in May the high school held their awards and scholarship ceremony. Cami, Justine, and the rest of the spirit team began, dancing to the "Believe It or Not" song, about walking on air, feeling free, flying away, and believing in oneself. That brought the audience standing and cheering. The positive vibes from the music helped accentuate the importance of the ceremony.

Cami stood as her name as well as that of other seniors got called as recipients of the HOPE scholarship. She looked to her left and saw Justine standing in a row ahead of her.

"God bless and keep Justine, she needed this scholarship so much," Cami mouthed. She smiled; sudden tears came to her eyes, the significance of Justine's need almost overwhelmed her for a moment.

Cami found Aunt Bea and Indella standing in the back of the gym after the ceremony. Justine weaved her way through the crowd and joined them. The teens hugged as the ladies looked on.

"I'm so proud of you, Justine, your ticket to the university," Cami whispered.

"I can hardly believe it myself," Justine spoke out the strangled words. They separated, tears streaming down their faces. They held hands and turned to Bea and Indella.

The ladies clapped for the teens, who were about to graduate and move forward with their lives. The four of them hugged.

4

"The end of the trail's ahead. I wanna sit down and talk, Cami. Over there," he pointed, "the grove of trees nearby. We'll have a little privacy."

Cole held Cami's hand as they headed off to the left.

"Tell him," Cami admonished herself.

They sat, drinking the warming water and eating the special trail mix Cami brought.

Cole eyed Cami and shook his head, "What is it in the trail mix that tastes, uh, just yummy?"

"The chocolate chips, little ones, they just add to the taste of the nuts and cereal."

"Are you ready?"

"Absolutely, been plannin' this time for a while, Justine also."

"Cami, it's scaredy-cat time for me." He shook his head and Cami watched the serious look on his face. "I've had this super nice life, smooth, no hiccups, not like you've had. Headed out, for really the first time in my life, on my own. God's beside me, he's still letting me freak about my future."

"When I get like that, and it doesn't happen as much as it used to," Cami touched his shoulder, "I keep saying, let go and let God. Sometimes I have to say it dozens of times, before I relax and let go of the worry, whatever it is."

"I'll meet new ladies, and new guys."

"Cole, say that to yourself over and over again."

He did, five times.

"Better?"

"Yeah, I guess."

He moved closer to Cami. She turned her head to him and he caressed her lips with his. They kissed and kissed, again and again. Cami felt a knife-like pain in her groin. The hurt caused her to flinch.

"My body says I want you, Cole."

"Yeah, I got a fearsome ache in my penis, for you."

They moved a bit away from each other.

"Can't do this, Cole."

"I know."

He looked into her green eyes, a deep green now, "You're my beautiful one, my very special one, Cami."

"I love you, Cole."

He paused, really hearing what she said, "And I love you."

They talked about their schools, Tech for Cami, State for Justine, and the U of G for Cole. They knew they needed time apart.

"It's the only way we'll know, time away,"

෴

Cami called ahead to let her know when she would get home from Tech. She listened to Aunt Bea's tired-sounding voice.

"Somethin's not right with Aunt Bea," Cami whispered as she carried her bags up to her bedroom. From there she went to her aunt's bedroom and saw her propped up in bed, papers placed around her. She gave Bea a soft hug and looked her in the eye.

"Working at home today. This's a kinda rush project, I'll go in tomorrow. I know, I know, you didn't see a tree in the living room when you got in. Oh sweetie," Bea burst into tears.

Cami made room on the bed and sat next to her aunt. She put her arms around her.

"Can you tell me?"

"I'll try, but first, finals, semester complete?"

"Uh huh, all done, so relieved, done real good."

Bea remained quiet. Cami heard her heave out a big breath.

"I've got a bad kidney, a disease, inherited, PKD."

"And that is?"

"Polycystic kidney disease, uh, lots of cysts on my kidney, not cancerous, but they've pretty much taken over my kidney."

"On the other kidney, the PKD?"

"Yep, starting."

Cami stood up and took hold of her aunt's hand. She looked directly into her aunt's eyes.

"You need a new kidney."

Bea nodded her head to Cami.

"You go back to work; I'll fix our favorites for dinner."

"Thank you, my darling girl."

"You're welcome; you've been there for me for all these years. Now, right now, and in the future, I'm here for you, Aunt Bea. Do you understand me?"

"I do, and I am grateful."

Cami began in her bedroom and sorted out clothes from her bags for washing and others for hanging up. Tears caused her to stumble as she took dirty clothes down the steps for washing. When she got to the laundry room, she found Aunt Bea's dirty clothes dumped on the floor, at least three loads.

"Oh dear God, she's really sick, God, how can I help her?"

She knelt down among the dirty clothes and cried out, "I can't lose Bea. She's the most important person in my life."

She continued to kneel and then she swore she heard the little engine chugging, from a favorite book of her childhood that she read time and again to her mom.

She remembered, "I think I can, I think I can, I think I can, as the little engine steamed up that high old hill."

Cami got up, wiped her face and nose, and began to sort through both her and her aunt's clothes. She started the washer and proceeded from room to room in her aunt's townhome.

"This is bad, really bad, oh Aunt Bea," Cami whispered as she saw the kitchen with dirty dishes piled high, the living room with cans, dishes, and papers strewn about. She looked out in the garage. It looked like her aunt had not taken trash out for the trash man for a month.

"This is not my aunt at all; she is so sick all she can do is go to work. I wonder if they know?"

Three hours later Cami checked on her aunt. She slept, her papers still lined up across the bed. Cami woke her, "Aunt Bea, I'm headed out for a little bit, to get a few things."

Her aunt nodded her head to Cami, and then closed her eyes. Before she walked out the front door, she looked over her efforts, everything tidy as her aunt always had it before, for her and for Cami. She still had a load of wash to do and two dishwashers full of dishes, but Cami felt better about Aunt Bea's place.

She stopped at her favorite Christmas tree lot.

"I'm late this year, just got home from Tech; do you happen to have a just right little four footer for my aunt and me?"

George gave her a big grin, "Glad you're home, little gal, and yeah, I thought of you, but kinda got worried, like maybe you wouldn't get home."

"I'm here. Please show me what you got."

George pulled out a tree he had set aside, not for sale. Cami approved of it. He sawed off a little of the tree trunk so she could put it in water in the tree holder.

"Thank you George, you positively made my day, Merry Christmas to you and your family."

He helped her put the tree in her trunk. It stuck out a little, so George tied down the trunk with her cord.

As she made her way around the familiar grocery store, she felt a lump of sadness form in her throat. It felt like it would choke her, but she kept swallowing until the feeling subsided. A smile came to her face as she brought the little tree and the groceries in to her home. She set the tree in the corner near where they always placed it. After she put the groceries away in the pantry and refrigerator she continued her dish cleanup, placing clean dishes away and loading up the dishwasher.

She headed upstairs and heard her aunt in the shower.

"That's a good sign, I'll go make us coffee and start our soup and sandwiches.

Cami found the two boxes of Christmas decorations and brought them out along with the tree holder. Once she got the tree lined up and placed in the holder she started decorating it, the lights first. Cami watched as her aunt came down the stairs, holding the handrail, and walking with careful steps.

"Oh Cami, such a pretty little tree, thank you. And fresh coffee, how wonderful, I feel better, needed that shower."

Cami came to her aunt and they hugged.

"I cannot even express how worried I am about you, Aunt Bea, and not a word, I had no idea. Who knows?"

"Indella, my boss and fellow employees at work, Jake, and of course Chet. Justine doesn't know. Nope, there wasn't any reason to worry you young folks."

"Help me put on a few ornaments?"

Bea nodded and hung ornaments.

In the next half hour Cami assisted in moving all the papers from Bea's bed. She lined them up in a corner of the now clean kitchen island.

"I'll be all set for tomorrow, just scoop them in order, into my satchel."

Cami washed two more loads, including Bea's sheets and pillowcases.

They got ready to sit down to dinner at the dining room table.

"Thank you Cami, for doing the sheets."

"You maybe don't remember, but when I got so sick from my ear and the bad reaction to penicillin, you helped me, sheets, and all. It was such a nice feeling to scoot in to the fresh-smelling stuff."

"I have no plans for Christmas. I told Jake and Indella, maybe come over in the afternoon for dessert."

"What about mass, Bea?"

"Not midnight, maybe you should go alone, to the early service on Christmas Day, if I can't make it. I'll surely try. This food tastes wonderful."

"Yeah, good old tomato soup and toasted cheese sandwiches."

"Uh huh, you do them like I always do, in the fry pan, with loads of butter to make them squishy inside and out."

Cami laughed, "You taught me well."

Her heart warmed as she watched her aunt's eyes light up and a tiny smile come from her lips, for the first time since Cami arrived home that early afternoon.

"Want a fire in the fireplace?"

"Not tonight, please Cami, I'd just like to sit in front of this fine tree, tucked in with my blanket, and maybe Christmas music on the cd player."

Cami felt exhaustion creep into her back and legs as she put the last clean dishes away, the kitchen fresh and uncluttered, as always. She brought up the last load of wash and made Bea's bed. She peeked into Bea's bathroom. Cami checked off the need to clean it. And she got a vomit-like feel in her throat as she looked at the top of Bea's bedroom chest. She counted seven different containers of medicines. Cami made a mental note to ask her aunt about the medications along with putting out all the trash, from the house and garage, for the trash man tomorrow. She also wanted to go to the library to do an on-line search about kidney disease. She hoped she could research her aunt's dilemma.

"I don't want to have the computer at home up with the kidney stuff. It's already on Bea's mind 24-7."

℀

Cami raced up the steps into the Ephrine library. She stopped at the desk of her favorite library assistant, Evelyn. They chatted for a minute, Cami updating her about Tech. Cami touched her shoulder, thanking Evelyn for her kind words about her future. She spent two hours at the computer and reading a dated medical description of her aunt's problem.

She put her head down, breathed in and out until she felt relaxed. She remembered the front writings in her writing journal. She raised her head and it came to her.

"Like dad wrote, life, yeah, my life's like a shadow that runs along into the sunset. I know what I gotta do, for me, for Aunt Bea."

She gathered her notes from the research she did. She waved to Evelyn on the way out and wished her a happy holiday season. When she got home she started coffee, hoping that her aunt got through her busy last day of work before Christmas. She started the tuna melts, and Justine arrived.

"I can't believe it's been since August, last time we saw each other."

They hugged and Justine added, "You got stuff going on at school even on weekends, classes, and projects."

"That's it, you got work, getting to the end of my school and yours, so it's team stuff for me, and so hard to get everyone together to finish projects."

After they ate and cleaned up, Justine asked about her favorite chocolate chip bars.

"Didn't have time, got home yesterday to a dirty, chaotic house, no time to bake."

Cami felt the hot tears spurt from her eyes, not able to contain her sadness any longer.   Justine felt her tummy lurch seeing Cami's distress.

"Girl, you sick? What's goin' on, come on."

"I'm, well, here; I'm sorry I'm being such a baby."

Justine's dark eyes pierced Cami's.

"It's Bea, right?"

"Uh huh, your mom may already know; they're friends."

"Uh, I don't know."

"Aunt Bea's got a kidney disease, almost destroyed one kidney, other one's starting to give her trouble."

"Horrible bummer deal," Justine began to tear up.

"She needs a kidney transplant; otherwise," Cami stopped talking. She broke down crying again. Justine came around the island and they hugged.

"You've researched this, I know you, Cami."

She nodded to her friend.

"It's about five years before someone can get a donated kidney."

"Yeah, lots will die who need it. What about friends and family of the person, you know, maybe who could donate?"

"Uh huh, I've read about that."

"Cami, what about you, you're family, the only person remaining in Bea's close family, her folks and brother dead."

"I'm seriously considering getting checked out to see if I could donate."

"Oh my goodness," Justine sat back down across from Cami.   "Oh, my friend," she paused, absorbing Cami's statement, "that would leave you with just one kidney, you willing to live with that?"

Cami nodded to her.

"Research?"

"Yeah, a lot, what I read is that the person donating, well, the remaining kidney grows, taking over the chore of the two kidneys. And my Aunt Bea, she's the most important person in my life; Justine, look at all she's done for me, since I was a sophomore in high school, losing my folks, all those years ago."

"I gotta go in a minute, Cami, mom'll be off her shift in a little while. And I've got lots to do."

"You just got in today?"

"Yeah, worked a late shift at the bakery, you know, holiday stuff."

"Maybe you and your mom can come over Christmas afternoon, for dessert."

"We'll see, hey, you always have a plan, tell me what you're doin' about your aunt."

"Yeah, a university in Atlanta has what seems to be the best kidney donation and kidney transplant center in this whole area. Actually, it's not that far from the Tech campus. I'm checkin' into it as soon as I get back for next term."

They stood and walked to Cami's front door together. They hugged.

Justine stood away from Cami and shook her head, "Challenges, oh girl, that's been going on for so long now. Between the docs, and God, you'll continue to figure this out for your aunt. I'm prayin' so hard, for you, for Bea, for what's to come. Merry Christmas, Cami."

℘

She picked up her cell phone and listened.

"Oh my gosh, Cole!"

"Uh huh, it's me, can I take you and Aunt Bea to midnight mass?"

"Just me, Aunt Bea, uh, what about your folks? Aunt Bea's not feeling well, lots I gotta tell you."

"We got the break, Cami. And my folks, they're happy about me seein' you and Bea, for mass or whenever we can be together."

"Maybe you get a good break from the U of G, but I gotta get back, special project I'm workin' on for one of my profs, gettin' credit, that's great news for me."

"What about the dorm, you can't get in yet."

"Stayin' at Justine's place, until the dorm opens. Yeah, I'll go to mass with you."

"Be ready at 11:15; we gotta be there by 11:30. The church'll be packed full."

"Then come back to Aunt Bea's; I'll make us early Christmas breakfast."

"And spill, whatever in the heck is goin' on with you, I'm concerned."

Cami heard the worried tone in his voice.

∓

"Thanks for meeting me out here, Cami"

She got in his car and they hugged. She hesitated, then raised her lips to his and kissed him. He gave her a caressing kiss back. Cami wasn't sure how much of the mass she comprehended, but she sang in a coordinated alto voice, harmonizing with the main melody of "Silent Night." She remembered Cole holding her hand through the whole mass, except when they went to communion.

"Bacon duty, or eggs?"

"I'll do the eggs, you microwave the bacon, right?"

"Yeah I do, didn't know you knew that. How many year's it been?"

"Wow, since 2003, 10 years, long time Cami. My friend, my neighbor, those play times, so memorable."

He turned from scrambling the eggs to see Cami's eyes tear.

"Whatever it is, wonderful friend, it's tearing you apart."

She nodded to him and continued to cook the bacon.

They ate and ate, downing the bacon, eggs, fruit, and several kinds of pastries.

"I'm starved."

"Me, too, Cami, talk."

She went on to explain Bea's illness, and what needed to be done.

"And I got a timeline, to see if I'm a donor possibility for my aunt."

"Tell me."

"One year from now, I'd need to take my spring semester off to donate, recover, take care of Aunt Bea. Then I'd do my internship in the summer, and go back in the fall, graduating, then a real job after Christmas."

"Step back a minute, Cami, you're assuming you can be a donor. You don't know that."

His blue eyes shone into her green ones, a question she saw in his eyes as they searched for more meaning.

She nodded her head, "That's right, I don't, but I'm a family member, and Aunt Bea and I happen to have the same blood type, if that matters at all."

"Yeah, I'm no doc, but I'm assuming that'd help."

"Let's clean up."

"Cami, this's huge, an operation, losing a part of yourself, are you sure?"

They dried the last of the pans and took their coffee into the living room. Cole put his arm around Cami as they sat, admiring the perfect shape of the little tree.

"You didn't answer me."

Cami turned to him after she took a gulp of her coffee.

"Bea's an angel, who took me in, when I was hurtin' so bad. I would absolutely be willing to give a part of me, for her. She gave me my life," Cami let out a big breath, "really she did."

"The donor process?"

"Go through paperwork, tests, both me and Aunt Bea. That'll take time. The wait for an outside donor is five years. She'll be dead by then. I gotta act now. School can hang on for a semester. I just gotta take an on-line class the semester I'm out so I remain in admitted status."

"That's right, dropping out," his lips thinned as he thought of the process of readmission.

Cami watched him as he held her hand.

"Can I try to see if I could donate?"

"Think you could get checked out."

"I definitely would do that for your aunt."

"Oh, Cole, you need to consider, real hard, about that."

"I will, I'll talk to my doctor dad, see what his thoughts are."

"Justine and I've talked. She asked about checking to be a donor. I told her absolutely not. She's in nursing, and needs all her body parts, working with sick folks all the time, and the terrible hours she'll have to endure. Health folks, they're super special."

"Yup, they are, a perfect profession for Justine." He paused, ""My mind's spinnin', Cami. Donor testing, all that stuff, where does that take place?"

"Right in Atlanta, not that far away from the Tech campus. You're in Athens, you'd have to come over when you can, to be tested. I know Justine could put you up at her place; I'll stay in the dorm until I'm graduated."

"I can see all this so clear; your aunt's gonna get help. She'll go on to have a good life, uh, she and Jake?"

"I think, serious, this whole situation's really whacked them out."

"Never seen more plainly, God's purpose in our lives, gettin' soon startin' on our careers and helping sick folks. We sure as heck are not alone; our faith, it sure is a special force in our lives."

She nodded, "In thinkin' of Aunt Bea, really lucky for me, I've only been sick once I can remember."

"Yeah, your ear and voice, and your bad reaction to medicine."

Cami turned to Cole and nodded, "One of the lowest times of my life, besides mom and dad dying, you helped, and 'course Aunt Bea stood with me every step until I recovered."

"So I see how much you want to help her."

They reached for each other, kissing each other, again and again. The pain of wanting each other simmered within them. Their tongues touched and ignited the wanting.

Cami finally pushed her hands away from his chest.

"I can't."

"Me neither, put your head next to mine, I'm wiped, too much to absorb."

"Right."

Cami stretched out and lay into Cole.

Bea woke with a start and heard quiet from the first floor. Putting on her robe she took slow steps down the stairs. She found the overhead stove light still on. Then she checked the living room with the white-lit tree shimmering from the outside street lamp coming in through the window. Cole and Cami lay together, sound asleep. Bea found a comforter and placed it over them.

"They gotta be so tired," Bea whispered, thinking about getting home from school and all the chores piled on them, getting ready for Christmas. "It's Christmas Day, thank you God, for giving me this day."

She gazed down on the two young people, "They're beautiful, the future," she whispered, nodding. She touched her hand over her heart, patting three times.

℘

He stood in front of her chair.

"Cami, hey, what're you doin' here? Didn't I just see you in class this morning?"

She watched him sit down next to her, his eyes wide in surprise.

"Back atcha, Greg."

Her mind raced ahead, as she asked, "What the heck are you doing in this place?"

"Seein' if I can donate a kidney."

"Me, also."

He shook his head to her, his brown eyes wide in concern, "When you're done, we gotta talk."

They met a while later in a little café near the donor center and sat across from each other, steaming coffee in front of them.

"You first, Cami."

She watched a worried look on his face, a handsome face. He worked on projects with her and several other classmates. He was the quiet one in that engineering site development class. She shook her head, and he saw the start of tears in her gorgeous green eyes.

"I, I guess we just don't know people; you shared only a tiny bit of yourself with the rest of us in the group when we started this semester. My Aunt Bea, she's my guardian since my folks died, she's got a bad kidney. And the docs, well the other one is starting to be affected," she shook her head as he saw her tears.

"So you're gonna see if you can donate yours."

"Right."

"My mom lost a kidney to kidney cancer. Her other one's so overworked," he paused and gave her a piercing look with his brown eyes, "how quick does Bea need a kidney?"

"Absolutely by January of next year, it's me, I gotta do next fall semester, the capstone, and then take one on-line class spring semester to stay admitted, donate if I'm able, recover, help my aunt for at least 6-8 weeks after. It's just her and me."

"My mom, her need's immediate. If I c'n donate, I'll still stay in school this semester. Mom has dad, and other family members to help her out when she gets home."

"Greg, you need a couple of weeks to recover, no driving, and all that stuff."

"I'll be OK; I've talked to my profs already; I'll catch up. They all understand how critical, what an emergency all this is, but that I still need to stay in school."

"Other family members seeing if they can donate?"

"Yeah, mom's sister, and my older brother."

"Any word yet?"

"No, we're pretty scared about all this; the cancer, sudden. The whole C thing's knocked the family for a loop."

"I'm not sleeping much at night. I'm it, for being a possible donor. Our other Ohay family is older and live in Canada. You know the wait for an outside donor's about five years."

"Yeah, mom won't make that."

He took hold of the hand Cami laid on the table.

She squeezed his hand, "Right, neither will my aunt."

They agreed to e-mail each other. Cami asked to follow Greg's progress if he were the donor for his mom. She felt confident, keeping up her praying to be a compatible donor.

5

Christmas a year later

And she was.

Cami brought the coffees after she gave everyone a piece of pumpkin pie with a dollop of whipped cream. She looked around Bea's living room, a bigger tree with colored lights this year. She felt a warm glow wrap around her as she watched Jake and Bea sitting close, having pie, with Chet in a chair nearby. Save for the crackling fire, it was quiet as they tasted the cinnamon and cloves addition to the pumpkin in the pie.

"Delish."

"It's Cami, she's been doin' that to pie since the first one she made, just a few months after she became my family."

"I'm ready for a second piece," Chet spoke out, "here's my empty plate."

"Yeah, this dude, what a sweet tooth," Jake said as they laughed together.

"Anyone else?" Cami asked as she got up to refill his plate.

"Two dollops of whipped cream, this time, please."

She fixed up plates for Chet and herself and returned to the living room. She stoked the fire and ate her second piece, savoring the special taste of the pie.

"We all set?"

"Chet, I guess as set as we'll ever be. I want to thank you so much, right now for what you're doing for this Ohay family. Just the fact that you're going to do a lot of driving, between Ephrine and Atlanta, that's so important. And Jake, your encouragement, caring so much for us, well."

Bea stopped talking, unable to go on. Jake held her hand and kissed her on the cheek.

Cami nodded, looking first at Chet and then at Bea and Jake, "Blessed beyond measure," she mouthed.

Cami cleaned up dishes after Chet and Jake left. Bea gazed ahead as she came into the kitchen. Cami saw that Bea's eyes weren't on her, but far away, in some other place.

"Having a hard time getting your head around all this, Aunt Bea?"

She nodded to Cami, "Actually the fear's subsiding, I just can't believe this's happened to me. Never really been sick, God's given me a curve ball. My religion's always been a steadying support in my life."

Cami came to her aunt and hugged her, whispering, "Not so steadying right now."

"That's for sure."

Cami kept a journal of Greg and his mom's kidney donation process, beginning with Greg's donation last January. From time to time Bea referred to it, giving her a sense of the reality of what would happen. The journal sat at a special spot on the kitchen island, for both women to refer to when they wanted.

"I'm so glad you kept a journal of the O'Leary's, I call it an adventure."

"It'll be our adventure coming up quick."

৪০

"So super you decided to join us for our before New Year/after Christmas time in our mountain home."

Cami looked over to Greg as they held hands. They hiked along the trail on the hills above the O'Leary place in the north Georgia mountains.

"I really need this, a time away, to get my mind square around what's gonna happen to my body, to my aunt's body."

"You've had quite a learning lesson from me and mom, paying attention to everything that went on, seeing me and mom in the hospital after the surgeries and following on for all this year."

"Yeah, your mom, she's a real miracle, a smile always on her face. And Greg, your recovery, it seemed quick, how's your body doin' after," she paused as he smiled to her, "it's almost a year?"

"Following all the docs' instructions, I was in decent shape before the surgery and I'm trying to eat healthy."

He shook his head, laughing, "Except this holiday time, really loaded up on fine food."

"Yup, your family loves their casseroles, soups, and stews, lots of new tastes for me."

That evening they sat in front of the toasty fire, downing the last of the mac and cheese casserole, and beef stew the family left for them.

৪০

"It's awesome we're together tonight. Tomorrow clean up and lock the cabin for the next trip my family makes up here." He paused, "Then you've got to head home."

They brought plates of the rich chocolate cake slathered with the whipped white frosting to the fire.

"A new tradition, I learned from your family, this cake, the Baby Jesus birthday cake, I'm Catholic, but hadn't heard of doing the cake."

"Yeah, it really made sense when us kids were small; we could relate to birthdays, more so than a baby being born. It took several years to understand how important Jesus, the Son of God, really was."

They watched the fire burn down slow as they finished the cake. Greg took the plates from them, setting them aside. He scooted next to her, touched her cheek, and plied her lips with his. Soon their tongues touched, the taste of chocolate, a delight. Cami shuddered at the sharp ache building in her whole groin area.

"Your wanting?" he whispered.

"Oh my," she whispered back.

"I've loved you, Cami, since I watched you sitting in the donor waiting room. Somehow I knew you were doing something very important. I guess, all along, in the classes we've had together, there's something caring, good, sensible about you."

"And you, always the quiet one, I've found out you aren't really always silent, like away from the classroom and the projects. You love your family so much; I only got that loving look from my mom, and then from my aunt. Your brother, mom and dad, and your bro's special friend, I've learned a lot from you. Cancer's such a burden."

"I call it a challenge, to let the docs and God do the work that needs to be done. And somewhere I've heard if you love hard enough, anything is possible. That for sure is my family."

"I've always thought you were special, but it was after the donation surgery, you laying in that hospital bed, a confident smile on your face, not long after you got out of recovery. It was what you were willing to do, you being an example to me. That's when I knew I loved you."

Greg stood and scooped her from the floor. He carried her to the bedroom and lay her on the bed. He took off her shoes and sat on the other bed, untying his own.   They lay together on the single bed in the room Cami shared with Jenn, Harley's girlfriend, during the holiday time.

They lay side to side, gazing into each other's eyes.

"Cami, I want you to be a part of my adventure, of my future, one day to call you my wife."

"For our one day, Greg."

They took their time undressing each other, kissing and savoring their new found intimacy.

"I've never," she whispered to him.

"I'm not far behind you, we'll share this together."

They rocked into each other as he took his time entering her slickness.   He thrust slow, slow, until his semen burst inside her.

They lay together after Greg helped wipe blood and semen from her.

"I'm so happy, Greg, that we shared this experience.   I was scared."

"I know, never seen that side of you."

"But I do have that side, when stuff's new for me."

They spooned together and slept.   And in the morning they showered, taking their time soaping each other and rinsing off.   As they towel dried Greg whispered to her, "When your lovely hair is lined with silver, I'll still love doing this with you."

They held tight to each other as they walked from the bathroom to dress.   Cami traced his scar from his kidney donation.

"Very soon you'll have a scar like this."

"Yes, I will, counting so much on Aunt Bea's recovery, like your mom's."

Cami helped Greg close down the cabin, readying it for the next trip the family would take here, for Valentine's Day or Easter.

"Let me buy us breakfast on the way back to your home, Greg.   Then I'll hop in my car and make the dash back to Ephrine for New Year's.   I find it so hard to believe I'll only be thinking about an on-line humanities class for this coming semester."

As they sat in the diner near Greg's hometown, he answered back.

"You've got an important, life-giving item to deal with."

"I do, but, thanks to you, I'm as prepared as I think I can be."

ℰℴ

"I'm home," Cami spoke out as she let herself.

"Upstairs, sweetie."

Cami heard the croaking sound of her aunt's voice. She hung her bag over her shoulder as she hurried up the stairs. She set the bag in the hall and watched her aunt put up her hand as she started to walk into her room.

Cami felt sweat dotting her forehead as she saw her aunt with a tissue over her nose.

"Week delay, the doc wants me to get over this cold before we head to Atlanta."

"How'd this happen?" she shook her head to her aunt.

"Probably mass, there's been a lot of sickness in our town. Work, the folks are healthy there, but you know, church, all ages, everyone crammed in together for the Christmas celebrations."

"So everything's been rearranged, both our surgeries, and all the other stuff." Cami stopped and asked, "Oh, you let the recovery home know, that we'd be delayed?"

"Right, Melden House, they'll take us whenever we're ready to leave the hospital, well you'll go there first, and depending on how I'll recuperate, I'll follow on. Between Jake and Chet, we'll get driven around wherever we need to go."

"Yeah, it'll be good when I get home, one less hassle for them in Atlanta."

"I think Chet will be doing the driving around for you, also Indella's going to help. Jake'll stay pretty close to me, will do some back and forth to Atlanta."

"Can I get you anything?"

"Please, coffee, and a pb&j, just on one slice, and I'll come down."

Cami set the coffee and sandwich out for her aunt and returned upstairs to unpack. She started the washing machine and circled back into the kitchen.

"Cami?"

"Yes, Bea?"

"Got a call earlier; your grandparents are making a quick trip here to see us tomorrow afternoon. They'll go back for their own church activities the next morning, so staying overnight."

"OK with that, uh," Cami paused and tried to remember, "you ever met them?"

"No, they wiped Priscilla completely from their lives, in Africa for all that time you were growing up. I'm completely OK with them visiting. They think what you're doing for me, well, saving my life, for sure. Continuing to mend fences, Cami, you've become very special to them."

Cami smiled to her aunt as she sat at the kitchen island, savoring a little more coffee.

"I see the ham in the frig."

"Uh huh, that'll be the meal for tomorrow night. If I'm better, I can help you prepare the meal. We'll keep it simple."

"Green bean casserole, salad, did you get a cheese cake?"

"I did, and a can of cherry pie filling, in case anyone wants more yummy on top of the cheese cake."

"Right, oh Aunt Bea, you're always thinkin' of our tummies."

They laughed together. Cami came to where Bea sat and hugged her.

"I have such a good feeling about what's going to transpire between our bodies."

"So do I; Cole also called to wish us well in the donation process. I remembered to thank him for getting tested to see if he could donate. I know he was disappointed that he couldn't stand in for you."

"That's my friend, my Cole, concerned about us as he's been for all these years."

"Cami?"

"What?"

"He also shared that he brought home a special friend, female, to meet his family."

"That would be a serious step for Cole. Next one's his last semester. He's moving on, and I'm so glad."

"You have Greg," Bea nodded to her and smiled

"I do," she spoke out as she remembered her quiet, special, loving engineer who cared so much for his family, and for her.

ℂ

Having dinner with her grandparents and Bea the next evening helped Cami further understand this couple who were new to her life. They told Bea of their church addition and fix-up of the front entrance to their small church. The grandparents heaped praise on Cami for her help in spending that five days of her school break with them.

After breakfast the next morning the four of them held hands in a circle as Granddad Jacob prayed for the two women, one who would donate, and the other who would receive. Cami walked them out to their car and hugged each of them.

"You are our very brave and very strong granddaughter. God will continue to watch over you, and Aunt Bea. You are in our thoughts and prayers, Cami. We'll stay informed; Chet will call us."

Each grandparent took one of Cami's hands and squeezed it gently, smiling to her. After she saw them off, she walked back to her home. Stinging tears burst from her eyes, and for a moment she felt overcome.

"Look how far I'm come with them, look how far," she shook her head in disbelief. "God, keep us all safe, in your loving arms, through these next days."

She plopped down on the one step before the front door. She put her head down on her knees and cried. In a little while she raised her head and turned the knob on the front door.

"Not scared any more, I'm ready."

ℯ⁗

"Cami?"

"Ooohhh, the anesthetic, now I got my eyes open and can feel again, makin' me flippin' dizzy and out of it. I feel a covering on my tum."

"I'll note what you say about the drugs you've been given, your reaction," the recovery room nurse said.

"How soon can I just go on acetaminophen?"

"Very soon, since other stuff really bothers you."

"My Aunt Bea?"

"Knew you'd ask, she's still in surgery and yours went well."

"Back to my room, soon?"

"Yes."

Cami closed her eyes. When she opened them again, she saw Jake standing near the door of her room. She gave him a little smile and tried to wave.

"Welcome back, Cami."

"Hi Jake, Aunt Bea?"

"In recovery."

"What time is it?"

With Jake's answer, Cami realized that quite a few hours passed since her surgery started.

"You're awake," the nurse commented as she entered the room. "We'll ask your guest to leave. Tomorrow will be a great time for you to return. You'll see a remarkable change in this young lady," she smiled to Jake.

ॐ

By mid-morning the next day the nurse spoke the truth. Cami stood, in her bright blue robe over the hospital gown. She looked out the window at the Atlanta skyline. The staff removed all tubes and oxygen from Cami. She went to the bathroom, her remaining kidney working. She had a soft food breakfast and took a walk around the surgical ward with an aide who made sure she stayed on her feet. In 24 hours she could transfer to Melden House, and stay there for a time as she recovered with other kidney donors. Each day she would return to the hospital to be checked on her progress. Then Chet would take her home to Ephrine.

"I'm anxious to start on my on-line class," she spoke out.

When she was allowed, she walked to her Aunt Bea's room.

"You look grand, Cami."

"And I'm feeling better, most every hour."

"And you, Aunt Bea?"

"Not so good."

"What's happening?"

"The docs aren't sure; time, Cami, to see if my body will accept your kidney. They've got me on a lot of meds, and I feel nauseous, not wanting to eat much of anything."

"I'll let you rest and stop by later."

That afternoon Cami had a visitor, Greg.

He hugged her after she swung herself to the side of her bed.

"So good to see you, a non-medical type person. You got a break from class, nice."

They laughed together after Cami shared.

"Uh huh, I felt the same way about day two of my donation time, in the hospital."

"Greg, so many of my dreams, after losing my folks, have come true. But this is the biggest dream, to see my auntie recover. I saw her a while ago, and I don't know."

"Babe, it's really too soon to tell; I had the same worry about my mom. Us young folks, we expect instantaneous results for everything in our worlds. This one's gonna take time, as I found out."

"Yeah, I know that from my writings in the journal I did about you and your mom's recoveries. But it's different when it's me going through it."

"Right, let me help you with your robe. Wanna go see your aunt?"

"Let's."

They walked to Bea's bed. Cami noticed again all the tubes and wires coming from and to Bea's body. She hadn't remembered all of them from yesterday in her room. Bea's head turned to one side and she slept, the oxygen tubes into her nose giving her the help she needed.

They stepped out and walked down the hall.

"I don't like her coloring, so pale," she gripped Greg's hand.

"Time, Cami."

❧

Cami moved to Melden House after the docs pronounced her ready to leave the hospital. She would return each day to be checked. Soon her stitches could come out. What she liked about the house was that everyone there was a recovering donor or a recovering donor recipient.

She ate meals with several different families and began to feel a special bond with the donors. After lunch on Day 4 of her recovery, her second day at the house, she had two visitors in her room.

"Jake, hello, I can hug you, gentle-like."

Cami stepped away from him after they hugged and looked at his ashen face, the worry lines on his forehead. She glanced at the other person, an official at Melden House.

Vomit shot up her throat as she started shaking her head. Her mind whirled, "So many dreams, come true." She'd shared that with Greg when he visited her.

"Tell me."

"Bea's body's rejecting the kidney."

Cami crumpled on her bed as she felt stinging tears.

"I engineer-speak, math please."

"ICU, she's there now."

"Percentages?"

"Immuno-suppressing medications, to help with rejection, aren't working."

"Cami," Mrs. Sheridan spoke, "they're trying a different regimen of medications. It's all gonna take time."

"50-50, whether she makes it or not, 'specially if her other kidney shuts down, am I right?"

Cami's bright green eyes pierced the official's.

"Can't say, exactly, time, Cami."

"Can I see her?"

Jake shook his head to Cami, "Not a good idea, she's pretty out of it, on a respirator. It'll upset you and you're in recovery, just not in the hospital."

"Oh my God, dear God, on a respirator, that's, that's. Jake, please stay, I gotta talk to you. And thanks, Mrs. Sheridan for bringing him to see me."

Cami felt her face flush and a little dizziness overcome her. She took some deep breaths. She tried to remind herself that she was just a few days away from abdominal surgery and a kidney removal.

"I need coffee, if you could get some for both of us, and a discussion."

After they left the room, Cami grabbed her notebook. She set it aside for her on-line class, in case she had time to start it, before she left Atlanta.

"Thanks, Jake, I needed this."

She sipped the coffee.

"I know you gotta get back to the hospital; right now we're living a dream of some kind. You know this's outa our hands. You know that?"

She gazed at him until he acknowledged what she said, with a nod.

"Don't know if Aunt Bea and you've talked, but she and I have. We knew the rejection would always be a possibility, now, and even later. Each day she lives, that I live, it's gift from God."

"That's right, Cami."

"While you were out getting coffee I started a list in my notebook. This is a difficult discussion, but I gotta."

She watched Jake nod to her and his eyes fill with tears. She sat upright on her bed, her knee raised so she could write in her notebook and read her notes.

"Please pull a chair close. This talk with you; never been more clear to me about Aunt Bea, making it," she paused, took a deep breath, "or not."

Jake saw her quiet face, devoid of expression, her lips in a thin line.

"You didn't really know me, except at the stables, but at 14 my folks were gone. Aunt Bea rescued me. I observed her through all the steps she had to take in settling my parents' affairs. Jake, it was a mess," Cami shook her head to him, "my dad losing everything in his stocks. I lost my home, school, everything I'd always known, dad's debts. Now I can see so plain that, all these years later, I'm a stronger, better person than the spoiled brat rich kid I was.

So I know if I have to, I'll sell Bea's townhome, settle all her debts and affairs, I'm on her car title, have a key to her safety deposit box and am the beneficiary on her 401K and life insurance. I'm her personal representative, that's what her will dictates, and believe me, working with estates at her law office, she's totally got everything about her life under control."

"That's great, Cami, because she kept her personal life away from me. So I've felt so hopeless about her, especially the last couple of days. But I can see that the two of you."

He stopped talking and put his head in his hands. Cami let him cry it out.

"The one thing she can't control, the kidney, that's killin' me," he sobbed.

"Me too, the helplessness, Jake."

"So it's kinda a relief that her life's in order."

"Will you be heading to Ephrine?"

"Right, the docs, there's nothing I can do here, except pace and worry."

"Everybody says it's gonna take time; you've got your work at the stables."

ᏸᏅ

The next day Cami went in to the donor center to be checked. Everything seemed fine in her recovery process. The staff thought she might be able to return home after several days, instead of the usual two weeks. Cami stopped by ICU and talked to Bea. She noticed her aunt got the respirator removed.

Hearing Bea's soft breathy voice helped Cami understand how much the surgery affected her. She did not smile, but she patted Cami's hand when Cami told her how well she progressed toward returning home.

"I love walking back to Melden House. I get stronger with every walk."

She stopped at the hospital chapel before she started her walk. Cami had a chance to talk to God and to thank Him for the recoveries.

The next morning after breakfast she got out her laptop. After several hours of working she decided she liked the humanities class, so different from everything she knew in engineering. The front desk called the phone in her room.

The receptionist asked her to come to the lobby, that she had guests.

That morning she curled her long hair, letting it flow over her shoulders in front and down the back. She wore her favorite Tech sweatshirt, blue jeans, and comfy pink slippers.

"Gosh, I wonder who it could be, guests?"

She stopped by the front receptionist who pointed out that her guests were in the welcome area. She smiled as she approached two tall men, who stood talking at the windows looking out on the patio and garden area. Cami pattered toward them. She stood stock still and gasped.

Each of the men moved toward her, one dark-haired and dark-eyed, and the other, a blue-eyed blonde.

"God, help me," she swallowed hard as she looked to them, "I never dreamed this would ever happen."

"Cami, I'd not have suspected surgery was such a short time ago for you," Greg thought.

"She's more beautiful, than I ever remember, oh Cami, oh my dear," Cole mused.

Cami walked to Cole first and he hugged her gently. She turned, moved to Greg and he hugged her gently. She put her hand to her cheek as she felt the flip-flopping of her tummy.

"I, I need to sit down."

They joined her at the round table with three chairs.

"Coffee?" Cole asked.

He always read Cami's face; she looked in distress, her eyes too bright right now.

Cami nodded, and Greg answered, "Yes, please, black."

"Black for everybody?"

Cami and Greg nodded to Cole.

Both men helped with the coffee and brought the paper cups back to the table. Cami took a sip of the hot brew. She took a deep breath

"I, I didn't know either of you were coming, oh my gosh."

She felt the flame rise from her neck to the top of her head.

"You two, you introduced yourselves."

Cole smiled, "We did, and we were equally surprised to be visiting the same donor. I tried to call your cell phone, but it musta been turned off."

"I just showed up here, Cami, 'cause I need to head to the lab to work on a project with some students you know. Our group just keeps getting smaller and smaller as we advance."

"And I'm here to visit you and then I'm hearing Bea's having a hard time; I'll go to the hospital after we visit."

"So, guys," she looked from man to man, "Cole's my buddy from our childhoods, grew up next door neighbors."

He spoke to Greg, "I'm a senior, accounting, at UGA. I'm going on, for my masters, and then study for the CPA, the masters necessary to go for the CPA."

"Oh my gosh, I had no idea that you needed the advanced degree," Greg acknowledged.

"And Cole, Greg and I, we're students in the same engineering program at Tech. So we been doing projects as a group for awhile."

"Last year, I donated a kidney to my mom; that's how I really got to know Cami, 'cause we met on a personal level, outside of school at the kidney donation center."

"You both're surviving with just one kidney; that's kinda unbelievable. How're you doing?"

"Time will tell for me."

Greg nodded, "It's been a year for me, it took a while to get to feeling like myself again."

"I'll butt in; Greg stayed in school, kept up with his work, besides doing the donating, an incredible effort."

Cole looked from Cami to Greg, "God works in wondrous ways."

Cami stood and asked Cole to join her at the windows.

"I'll be back in a minute, Greg, thanks for staying."

Cami gazed out the window and blew out a large breath, "Cole, I'll be heading back to Ephrine soon."

"You got your class to do on-line?"

"Yeah, already started it here, plus care for Aunt Bea when she comes home. It'll be a busy time, but I owe my life to my aunt."

Cole touched her shoulder, "As she owes her life to you, Cami."

"You going to go see her now?"

"Yes. I love you, Cami," he said as he turned to her.

"Same, Cole," she nodded as she smiled to him.

"I'll go, call you on my cell to let you know how she's doing," he said as he kissed her on her cheek. "Things are good at school."

Greg watched them together, "That's some special caring between them, a real history," he mused.

Cami walked back to the table, at a slow pace, needing to take a pain pill.

"I'll walk you to your room, Cami. This's an emotional time for you."

They held hands as they walked along.

"Greg, Jake and I've talked; it's so up and down with Aunt Bea. I'm ready to carry on, whatever God decides. Extreme Unction, I gotta think about it, Jake knows, Aunt Bea, she told me, it's what she wants, in case."

"Yeah, we talked about it with mom, several times, oh Cami."

They stopped in the hall; Greg held her lightly by the shoulder.

"I need to be alone, and thank you for coming, Greg. Get to your project. It'll be a wild ride, the rest of this semester for you."

"God bless and keep you, Cami. Struggles will continue. You're strong."

She turned to him and he kissed her on top of her head.

ॐ

Day four since her dismissal from the hospital arrived. Cami progressed enough to returned home after a final checkup the next morning. Chet planned to pick her up for the ride back to Ephrine. Jake would arrive to see Aunt Bea later that same day.

The ICU called Cami to let her know that Aunt Bea's kidney had trouble and she was back in that unit. Again, the kidney started to reject the medications that worked well so far for Aunt Bea. Cami walked from Melden House to the hospital. She arrived at ICU and heard the tortured breathing of her aunt. Bea remained conscious. Cami took hold of her fingers and leaned in.

She whispered, "Going back on respirator; feel terrible, Cami, God's present and He's a comfort. It may be time; I sometimes feel the light."

Cami kissed her on her forehead and whispered, "Extreme Unction?"

She watched her aunt nod her head.

Cami held back as she watched as the nurses, doctor, and priest standing near performing their tasks.

"It's like a play, like I'm watching as they all come and go and act out their parts. The doc says they'll try yet a different regimen of medications, maybe third times a charm. He told Aunt Bea that, but I'm not sure she's still with us, in her mind."

"We need to leave. What your aunt needs is time, for this third round of different medications to help her new kidney," the nurse guided Cami from the room. "Sure you're OK to return to Melden House?"

"Uh huh, I know Jake will call to see how she's doing, supposed to come soon. And I need to walk."

"You were with her, Cami, that's all your aunt wanted, just you. You are unbelievably brave."

The nurse gave her a gentle hug at the nurses' station. The priest who performed the ceremony walked up to her.

Cami smiled to him and nodded. He grasped her hand.

"In God's hands," she whispered to him.

He smiled back to her, nodding and waving a goodbye.

"I feel so calm, steady, I know it's You, God, like You've always been, right here," Cami walked along, headed for the house, feeling stronger, every hour. "We're in Your hands."

She looked up into the gray Atlanta sky and nodded her head.

∞

"Ready to head home?

"I am, I said my goodbyes to Aunt Bea yesterday, before the priest began."

Cami slept most of the way back to Ephrine, a city in the middle of Georgia, her hometown. Chet carried her bag and backpack with her laptop into her Aunt Bea's home.

"I'll leave you now; Jake'll keep us informed, as he'll stay another day near Bea. They've made up a sleeping bed for him, since he's spent so much time with her."

Chet gave Cami a gentle hug.

"Still several days before you're driving, right?"

"Uh huh, but I'm anxious to get out and about. I'm so glad to be home. The walking in Atlanta, back and forth from the house to the donation center, it felt great. But I know I've lost a lot of strength."

Chet stepped back from Cami, "Your body, major surgery, losing a part of yourself, I think you can see now how much that's taken out of you. You're young, so you gotta figure how long it'll take for Bea, when she returns to us."

That night Cami got a call from Jake.

"I've just come from praying in the chapel, it's bad, the docs completely puzzled. I'm set up to rest in her room."

"Thanks, Jake, I'll try to sleep, back in my good old bed. I'm ready, whatever God decides."

Cami awoke with a start. She fell asleep sometime in the night and now turned, looking out the window at bright sunshine. Sunlight moved over her as she took her time getting out of bed.

She padded downstairs in her pink slippers and Christmas tree pajamas. She started coffee, looking around with nearly every object reminding her of her aunt.

"Jack hasn't called; don't know what that means. Bea, have you joined God in His glorious light?"

She sat, eating toast slathered with butter and strawberry jam. The phone rang.

"Cami."

She listened for a clue in the tone of his voice.

"Yes, Jake?"

"Bea flat-lined early this morning; they brought her back. She seems better right now. They want to take the respirator away, to see if she can cope without it."

"That sounds promising, you'll keep me updated. Hey, what a ride you're having, how are you?"

"Tired, never been through anything like this, for sure."

"Stay in touch."

Cami put her head down on the kitchen island. She felt ready, if Bea lived, how it would go down. And if she didn't make it. The agony, misery Cami knew she could endure it if she lost her aunt. She would put her affairs to rest.

"Thank you God, for making me take this semester off; I could'a never done what Greg did."

But then she remembered that Greg's mom did not have the kidney rejection problems with which Bea fought.

§

Cami drove her car, wanting to go to the trail she helped build.

"Just 10 minutes, is all I'll go and then come back. I know I really shouldn't be driving yet, but going feels wonderful," she told herself.

She breathed in the dead wood smells and rotten leaves on the trail. She looked up.

"There's the gray sky color again, like the sky's biding its time, trying to decide to cloud up or break out into sunshine," she spoke out.

Her mind swirled, memories of her parents, Cole, Justine, Greg, her classes at Tech, and Bea. Tears stung her eyes as she walked at a slow pace back to the trailhead and her car. Her struggles, conflicts of her life, continued to plague the calm she wanted.

At home she listened to Jake's message that Bea started to feel better, off the respirator, eating a soft diet, going to the bathroom with help. He told Cami Bea would call her after her sore throat started feeling better.

ᘒ

"Just a few weeks left for me, Cami, your aunt's doing well."

Greg turned to her as they walked along the park near Aunt Bea's home.

She looked at him, "Know where you're headed?"

"Took a job with Mourhouse; to Saudi Arabia on a monster building project, one year."

"Oh my gosh, that sounds like the sort of challenge you're looking for."

"It is, and Cami, when I return you'll have been on a job assignment for six months, so it'll be your chance to see how you like the world of engineering, using the skills you've learned at Tech."

"I won't be able to come to your graduation, Greg."

"How's that?"

"Belen wants me for the months of May and June, for my internship with one of the project managers."

"Where?"

"Mohave Desert."

"And you'll be doing?"

"Helping coordinate the completion of the solar thermal energy facility."

"That's a super sunny place, hot."

"Right, I'm getting prepared for that."

"Where'll you live?"

"Outside Searchlight."

"Uh, state?"

"Oh," she saw his questioning expression, "right, Nevada."

"Let's sit, over here in the grass. I gotta go in a little bit, back to Atlanta, but I wanted to spend part of a day with you. Where are we, as a couple, in all this?"

Cami shook her head to him and tried to smile after they sat down.

"Our timing's crummy, you're the right man, I love you, but it's the wrong time, at least in my life, gotta finish up at Tech fall semester, there's my capstone, and other classes. Then a job; be with a big group, like you're with, civil engineering, building somewhere in the world, like you're gonna do."

"Are we breaking up?"

She watched his face, stricken, eyes misty, and his forehead wrinkled.

"I love you so much, but Greg, I must let you go. You got such a bright future, with Mourhouse, they're a CE group, huge. It'd be your chance to really see the world. I'm so excited for you, graduation, and on."

"Will I ever meet anybody like you?"

She gave him her wide-eyed look, smiling and nodding to him.

"You will, in the world of engineering, the women, those out there, they're tough, driven, like I've got to become."

"You so caring, maybe, not gonna find that, willing to help out your family, like I helped my family. That's the kind of woman I desire. When I'm with you, Cami, you can't imagine how I feel when I'm with you," he paused and let out a deep breath, "happy, home."

She heard Cole's voice in her head from somewhere in their past, "You're my coming home, Cami."

Greg helped her up and held her hand as they walked back to Aunt Bea's.

"I'm not giving up, Cami, like with the donations, the surgeries, all that time. I'll get a handle on my career, then for you, for you to get started on yours. You're somewhere in my world."

They smelled coffee brewing when they arrived at Aunt Bea's.

Cami thought, "She's up; Greg really wanted to see her."

After Greg hugged Bea, Cami excused herself so they could spend a few minutes together. Cami sat on her bed, in the room, a refuge for her for a long time.

"Greg, so hard to do this. God, hope you're still with me, this's kinda like losing a loved one. Hey, I'm losing a relationship, but what I need now is friends, for some time to come," she mused as she looked at her calendar. In her mind she went over the next six months, then graduation and an engineering job somewhere out in the world.

She walked him out to his car. They hugged. She felt stinging tears as she looked into his wet eyes.

"Congratulations, graduation, and new position. God bless and keep you, always, Greg."

He whispered, "I love you, deep in my heart."

He kissed her forehead, and she touched his cheek. She turned and hurried back into Bea's home. She did not look back.

6

Cami gazed up and across.   She saw the trio of 450 ft. high power towers with each one topped by a 2200 ton boiler.   The heat shimmered around her, the little breeze like a blast furnace.   She found her way inside to the Benel construction office.   Her boss, Sandra, waited for her.

"Did you get your last good look?"

"I did.   What an awesome project to be a part of, the end of it.   I can only imagine what this piece of desert looked like, just the few years ago, as the company began the project."

Sandra laughed, "Just flat, little vegetation; it's come to life, this whole area.   And you're getting out of here, late June, before it gets any hotter.   I have a letter of recommendation for you.   Before you finish at Georgia Tech, you should take a serious look at our company.   You like big challenges, and whew, we got 'em, especially out of the country.   And you've heard this, we're seriously underrepresented in the woman engineer area."

Cami took the letter her boss handed her and put it in her portfolio case.

"Thank you, Sandra, I'll take off now; it's a long trek back to Georgia.   I've learned, oh my gosh, so much."

Sandra nodded to her as she stood and shook Cami's hand.

"Take care, be safe, let me know how your last semester goes. I like to keep in touch with former interns."

Cami drove into her aunt's neighborhood three days later. As she unpacked her car, her mind kept returning to the note she found on the kitchen island her first load in.

Cami, Yaay!! You made it home. I'm in the prelims of a project at work. I'd like to get your engineering expertise (you'll be reimbursed for your time). We'll talk; I'm taking you out to dinner tonight. Love, Aunt Bea

She tried to remember discussions in her classes about problems in construction. She nodded her head.

"There sure were," she spoke out, "the bridge ones I especially remember. But that's what I really want to do, work on bridges."

Cami worked off and on with Bea's law firm for nearly a month, finishing in time to begin her final semester at Tech.

ℰᴑ

"When do you head back, Cami?"

"Cole, whew, it's been awhile since we've talked. I go back, the old dorm, one last time on Friday."

"Someone I want you to meet; I'm engaged."

Cole heard silence on the other end.

"You still there?"

"I am, I, I, just had a 10 second rewind on our lives together, since forever. I'm forgetting my manners, congratulations, Cole."

Several days later Cami stood at the round table in the center of the little café. Cole rose and introduced the two women.

Cami gave Hope her wide smile.

"So, direct me, what's the plan, Cole?"

He looked at Hope, "See, I told you."

They smiled to each other as they held hands. The waitress brought coffee for Cami.

"Thanks, you guys, yeah, really know me, already ordered, coffee first."

"Right," she heard them say in unison.

"The plan is, as you always ask, Cami; I'll be finished with the Masters in late November, sitting for the Georgia CPA, by Christmas."

Cami directed her gaze to Hope.

"I work with middle school kids, science, coulda done more in science, but I love my kids."

"So you're STEM, like me," Cami nodded to Hope.

"I am; if I go on for a Masters, I might leave teaching. But it's pretty exciting, very lively, with youngsters in sixth through eighth grades."

"Uh huh, if we could only figure out how to channel all that energy," Cami laughed.

"Right," Hope beamed to Cami and then Cole.

Hope touched Cole's shoulder.

"I can see why she's such a special friend to you, Cole. She really catches a person up, with her sincerity, a bright light in people's lives, as you say."

"Oh, Cole, she loves you so; I see your eyes, though, you're perplexed," Cami thought as she gazed at him.

Cami filled in an awkward silence, "Your big day?"

"Can't decide, but probably sometime between Christmas and New Year's Day."

"Holiday weddings, so special," Cami smiled to them.

"Share about Benel."

"It's all engineer stuff, but I worked in the Mohave Desert, on a huge solar thermal energy facility. What was super cool is that Benel designed and built the project. From start to finish, it was theirs. This guy took three years; I interned with the engineer, a woman, in charge of the project completion. I guess my favorite part involved taking guests around to explain the workings of the facility. 'Course I first had to learn what went on for myself, before I could explain it in plain language to others."

Cami went on to describe Benel doing construction and civil engineering projects all over the world. This desert project finished safely, in the 36-month timeline set out. The solar panels on the ground generated power to the tower boilers. The electricity produced by the process would take care of 140,000 homes.

"I guess the weather conditions remained good, for all those months so work went on, day and night, at the facility site."

"A desert, sounds like it was a good place to put a solar facility."

"Right, great sunlight, and a huge number of solar panels."

"We're heading out. Hope's from Macon; we'll get married in her home church."

They walked out together. Cami hugged Cole and then Hope.

"God's with us all, good luck to you both and God bless."

"Thanks, Cami," Hope smiled to her.

Cami gazed into Cole's saddened eyes, the darkest blue she ever saw them.

"Oh dear God, he loves me, always has and always will. And I love him," she whispered as she walked away from them to her car.

Cami carried the final look Cole gave her, she carried that image with her for the next weeks. It haunted her.

"God," she prayed many times a day, "he shouldn't marry her. I don't think he loves her. But I can't butt in, not my place. It's just that I know him well, and for so many years."

She poured her efforts into long hours of studying; sometimes she decided she almost forgot how to study from being absent from school for a semester to help her aunt recover. By the middle of October she and her team in the Capstone class had their plan approved and well underway.

First, she and her team examined three different projects before they decided which entity they wanted to assist in helping with recommendations. Without much discussion they picked Cami's project, because it wasn't new to her, just them.

"It's what I helped my aunt with, a lawsuit involving a construction firm and a city, not far from Atlanta. A city bridge crumpled, long before it should have. Bottom line, the city decided to settle out of court with the firm."

Bea's law firm assisted in giving the students information they needed. From there the group met with the still-in-existence construction company and with the city. Her group spent time at the site, testing soil and taking samples of the concrete used in the construction.

During Thanksgiving week the group met for long hours, without the hindrance of having their other classes. Team members assigned themselves to the tasks of returning to the city, to the construction company and getting their project ready for the capstone presentations to faculty. Then all the projects would be on display for the entire campus to view.

On Thanksgiving evening the group got together for a potluck at Jed's apartment. Cami mainly listened until after they had dessert. Beer and wine flowed as they discussed their futures. Cami and two others in the group hoped to graduate in December.

"So, Cami, tell us about your future."

She looked from guy to guy, "Maybe you know, maybe not, I interned in May and June with Benel, on a Mohave Desert project, at the solar thermal energy facility. They finished up the three-year construction, and all systems ran great. So I'm on my second interview with Benel; it's where I want to work, with the biggest and the best."

"They're all over the world," Jed said. "Where?"

"I, well, not sure, but I think, a project out of country."

"Good luck," they all told her.

"Thanks."

ಜ

"The money, show me the money, the realistic money," the team heard that over and over again as they proceeded on to the completion of their project.

"It's the toughest thing we'll do, figuring the cost of the bridge replacement," they all agreed.

One of the team members created a budget for a project in another class. This group patterned their budget from his. Pete literally saved their butts.

When Cami could that presentation day, she walked around in the huge room in the student center, taking in all the different projects that the CE students worked on for the capstone.

"We'll help a lot of people, if they'll take our advice," she said when she returned to her group, watching the presentation they created loop again and again.

Throughout the hours they were there the whole group got to explain their project to people as they stopped and asked questions.   There was no doubt about the interest, a major bridge collapse made the news in Georgia.

As the semester ended, the capstone group split up. Some took their recommendations to the city and the rest spent time with the construction company. It would take effort to work out all the details, the insurance claims, and whether the city would ask the construction company to do the rebuild. Or the city might decide to go with another firm.

Cami sat with the Benel engineer recruiter at a round table in the Tech Career Center.

"So, how'd your capstone turn out, Cami?" Mr. Benjamin asked.

She studied him with her eyes. And she couldn't quite decide whether it was the fact that she was female or the demure outfit she wore. It just didn't seem like he believed what she said so far.

"I've seen that look, Cami.   Yes, I believe your accomplishments, two sentences about the capstone project."

"Soil testing and concrete, construction firm didn't take the research results for the soils seriously. The use of incorrect concrete and piling depths, well, the collapse."

"Benel wants you to come to work for us. In the first week of January we begin a project in Edmonton, Alberta, Canada. We want you on that team."

Cami blinked hard, then blinked again. He gave her preliminary details.

"When do I need to let you know?"

"By this time Thursday; uh, today's Tuesday, we'll assemble the team, then, on Friday. You're the only Tech student we're interested in, so no competition from fellow students."

She smiled to him as she rose, thanking him for his time, reiterating her desire to join the firm. Cami shook his hand as she repeated the date and time by which she would contact him.

"Finals, the rest of my life, coming up," Cami blew out a big breath as she walked back to the dorm.

ℂ

"Congratulations, Cami," Bea, Jake, and Chet said in unison.

She nodded to them as they toasted her with champagne at the little restaurant she loved in Ephrine. Only Aunt Bea came to the ceremony, at Tech. But she wanted this to be her big celebration, back home, with the folks she loved.

When she and Bea got home, Cami requested they have coffee and talk.

"I'm happy, Aunt Bea. We've come so far, since way back. Once I get to Canada I want you and Jake to be together."

Cami looked up and spoke, "You've waited long enough, mom and dad say so also."

"I want you to have a special Christmas with me, and our friends. It may be our last one, that we'll be together, for awhile."

"I need your help, Aunt Bea."

Bea nodded to her, "And I need yours."

"I believe this may meet your specifications, Cami."

She smiled to the salesman at the car dealership. She knew the vehicle she would need for her job. Aunt Bea stayed back in the reception area. Cami test drove two of the cars.

"I want to bring a friend who knows cars with me tomorrow. I need for him to check these two cars over. He'll need to get under the hood to look around, and under the car. Plus I want him to drive it, with me as passenger, so he can get the feel of it."

The salesman gave her a puzzled look, raising his eyebrows.

"That's a little out of the ordinary."

"So he can't look the cars over?"

"I'd have to check with my supervisor."

Cami's mind whirled, "This isn't gonna work," she thought.

She stood up from the chair, looked the salesman in the eye with her bright eyes, "I'm done here."

She walked with a quick pace out to her car with Aunt Bea and did not look back. She started to get in when she heard, "Miss, come back, please. I've got the go ahead from my super, bring your guy in."

Within three days, Cami purchased the 4wd car her mechanic suggested, complete with tires appropriate to Canada's winter roads. She traded in the clunker she drove all her years to Tech. She spent time at the emissions station and the county clerk's office. Aunt Bea helped her go through all the steps of vehicle purchase. Cami knelt in the driveway as she screwed on her shiny new Georgia license plate at the rear bumper. Bea clapped as she completed her task.

"There!" Cami exclaimed, "thank you for your help. You took care of everything for my last car. How can I ever?"

"Ssshhh," she hugged Cami, "I've loved every part of seeing you grow up, and I'm so proud of you, graduating and your job."

Later they stood, decorating a little bigger Christmas tree than last year.

"Aunt Bea, to let you know I sold the necklace, in Certificates of Deposit now. I've got a start setting up my future, getting an apartment in Edmonton, learning to deal with Canada winters, being outside in that cold."

"It's been so much fun helping you get all your Arctic gear on-line, hey go ahead and plug in the lights."

They stepped back from the multi-colored lights on the tree. Jake came in time for dinner, tonight hamburgers, fries, and salad. They sat together at the table covered with a red plaid tablecloth. Cami kept the CD player going with Christmas music.

"And for dessert?" Jake smiled to Cami.

"Cheese cake, of course, with your choice of chocolate syrup drizzled over the top, or blueberries, or, plain."

They all helped clear the table. Jake brought over the cups of coffee and Bea helped Cami with the cheese cake slices.

"Share with us your latest, Cami, you said you had news."

"Uh huh, gotta go to Oak Ridge, TN, for orientation to Benel. They're doing my work permit for Canada. Once that's finished they want me at the Benel office in Calgary. I'll be there for a few days, and finally will head to Edmonton. This project's a monster, will take years.

"What'll you be doing?"

"Preliminaries on additions to the light rail system in Edmonton."

"Bridges?" Bea smiled to her.

Cami laughed, "Obsessed with that all my life, uh huh, I'm sure there'll be bridges."

They finished dessert. Cami offered to clean up and sent Bea and Jake to the living room with their coffee. She peeked out as she washed the pots and pans and saw them sitting close together, watching the fire.

"Hold this memory, Cami, home, I hope I will be able one day to make a home like they plan to."

She let out a big sigh and headed upstairs to look over her plans for Oak Ridge and Calgary. She answered her cell at the fourth ring after she found it under a folder.

"Merry Christmas, Cami."

"Uh, Happy Holidays to you; who's this?"

"Cole."

"Oh, my gosh."

"Yeah, last person you expected to hear from, wanted to send my congratulations on your graduation."

"Thanks, hey what's goin' on; where are you?" she asked, her voice choking from the emotion of knowing.

"I'm not getting married; we broke it off two weeks ago, a horrible mess, invitations'd gone out. I'm in Atlanta; I've taken an accounting job with the state of Georgia, got a studio place. I finished up the Masters."

"So glad you've completed your studies, onward to your dream of the CPA. I'm so sorry, Cole, so sorry."

She stopped talking, trying to collect her thoughts.

"Gosh, I'm shocked." She paused, breathed deep; "You know me, what's the plan? Can I help?"

"Pray for me, Cami, pray for Hope. She's totally devastated. I couldn't live with myself any more. The love that we needed to go on; it wasn't there, from me. I'm to blame."

"Of course I'll pray for you both. In God's hands, Cole, He knows what He's doing. Right now, trust God, and His will for you."

"Thank you for reminding me, almost lost sight of Who's in charge."

"Your folks?"

"Super upset, and her parents, oh Cami, Hope's mom, I can't believe I almost married into that family. The words she said to me, that mom, it shook me to my core."

"Coming home to see your folks for Christmas?"

"Nope, I need time to get my life in order, after all the wedding planning and finishing up the degree. Cami, tell me your plans, where you're headed."

She went on to share her wandering way to her final destination job in Edmonton, through Oak Ridge, and then Calgary.

"I'm excited for you; that's gonna be some project, expanding light rail, and with the company you wanted to be with. Uh, didn't you intern with Benel?"

"I did, and I loved it."

"This's my phone number, and I'll stay in touch with you, Cami. You'll keep your same cell?"

"Not sure, lot's different in Canada, metrics, temperature, so I'll let you know once sea legs, so to speak."

She laughed and he joined in.

"It makes me feel so good to hear your laugh."

"Yours also, Cole."

℘

She cried a good deal that night, Cole, sad for him, future scary for her, whole different world, coming up for her. She kept flipping over in her bed, unable to sleep. At 4 a.m. she got up, brewed a pot of coffee and sat on the couch, gazing across at the bright Christmas lights on the tall tree. She prayed and remembered a night a few years back, when she and Cole fell asleep on that same couch.

"So much time, so many things happening, keep us in Your loving arms," she murmured.

She felt a touch on her forehead.

"Cami, sweetie, you OK?"

She opened her eyes and smiled to her aunt.

"Couldn't sleep, so made coffee, drank some, and watched the shadows catch on the tree lights. It musta put me to sleep. Are you up 'cause we gotta talk?"

"Me also, I've a special request."

Cami sat across from her aunt at the kitchen island.

"Your request, Aunt Bea?"

"I'm full-blooded Indian; you're half Siksika, Cami. I've done some research and found several family members of our dad, your Granddad Ohay."

"Wow, where?"

Bea saw the excited look in Cami's eyes.

"In the Calgary area."

"Calgary area, really?"

"Uh huh, don't know if you remember, but your grandparents lived on a Siksika Indian reservation, east of Calgary. They were born and raised there."

"Oh yeah, and they moved to Georgia, 'cause your dad got surveying work, right?"

"That's correct. His name is Charles Ohay, with his son, Robert, an uncle of mine and a cousin."

"So my great uncle, and second cousin."

"Right, and I've received a letter back from my uncle. I shared that you would be working in the Edmonton area."

"Did you tell him that I'd be at the Calgary office for a bit before they send me to Edmonton?"

"Yes."

"Oh, Aunt Bea, when I get time, while I'm in Calgary, I'd like to go meet him. That is," she thought for a moment, "I'll write him to see if he's interested in meeting me."

"Cami, I really think he'd like that."

"Does he know, about your folks, their deaths, and that dad was killed?"

"He does."

"Aunt Bea, I can sense, you have more news."

Cami filled their cups with hot coffee. Bea touched Cami's shoulder from across the kitchen island. She watched her aunt beam, her eyes bright and teary.

"February, Jake and I'll marry sometime that month. If it's possible for you to get away, I want you to be my maid of honor."

Cami came around to her aunt as she stood up. They moved away from her chair and jumped up and down, up and down, holding hands.

"Awesome, after everything you been through, your recovery, with me, and with us, Aunt Bea, to find love, a fine man, I also love Jake."

They hugged each other for a time as Cami started to cry. They stepped away from each other.

Cami held out her arm, "My tears, they're tears of joy, for you, for Jake, and for you together."

She sobbed and moved to hold Bea by the shoulder.

"I'm so happy for you and Jake."

ℴ‽

Chet and Cami danced, a slow waltz.

"I appreciate being able to come to New Year's with you, Bea, and Jake."

As he walked her back to their table, he turned to her, "Life, your career, will take you far from here, and very soon. My wish for you is that you have a grand life, and that you find more folks to love. I love you, Cami, and I am so proud of all you've accomplished. You absolutely gave your aunt her life back, I'm convinced of that."

"Thank you, Chet, I'll continue to make you proud," she smiled to him and nodded.

The talk at the table revolved around Bea and Jake.

"You'll still have a room, whenever you come home. Cami, we'll have a couch with a comfortable full-size pull-out bed in that third bedroom."

"A combo study and guest room."

"Right."

"Cami."

7

She heard a voice behind her and felt a touch on her shoulder.

"Hi folks," she heard him say to the others at her table.

"Oh Cole, it's good to see you," Aunt Bea nodded and smiled to him.

Cole shook hands with Jake and Chet.

"I'm taking this young lady away for a dance, please excuse us."

Cami continued to sit there, in dumfounded shock. In slow motion she scooted her chair back and took his hand. He helped her get up.

"Oh my goodness, never seen you in a tuxedo, wow, Cole."

"And that long black dress, wow back at'cha, Cami."

They held hands as they walked to the small dance floor.

"I, I."

"Yeah, just a rare spontaneous moment for me, decided to come home. I wanted to talk to my parents. They saved a spot for me here at the club, in the hope I might show up."

"And you have."

"Keep this vision of her in your mind, Cole, for another time that I may see her," he told himself.

"Excited about moving on?"

"Yes."

Cami felt his arms holding her close, in a slow dance. She floated along, trying to comprehend his being with her. They danced, and talked, and drank a little champagne, and danced some more.

"Feeling a little more comfortable with me?" he gazed down at her, his blue eyes darkening as he spoke.

"Awkward, Cole, I've known you for so long, this is hard for me. I'm still in shock that you're here."

She gazed around at the red decorations, red balloons, red crepe paper and netting, "And this room, it's decorated much like my mom did it one year. She brought me here to help her."

"So many memories, of my folks, of you, Bea and soon, Jake."

"That's right, oh Cole, so much whirling around in my head, questions, but I've got to get my professional life going. We'll be far apart, Edmonton, and Atlanta."

"We have e-mail, and our cells. And Cami, what I'm gonna go through for awhile is rebound stuff, I need to date, to clear my head, and figure out where I'm headed."

"Hey, that's the right attitude you've got. I've just had a few dates, since I told Greg we wouldn't be together."

They stayed on the dance floor for another dance; soon they would count down to the New Year. Cami and Cole kissed a quiet kiss, after the New Year began.

"God bless and keep you, Cami," Cole said as he hugged her.

"And God bless and keep you, Cole, our futures, so bright," she smiled.

&ᴐ

Cami got her transfer notice, so she could move from Calgary to Benel's Edmonton office. On her last weekend in Calgary she got acquainted with her great uncle. She agreed to meet him at a café near the reservation. Bea provided her with several pictures of her grandparents, at a much younger age. Clarence recognized her immediately, tall, with her skin a milky tan, and incredible green eyes. She could not find him in the restaurant until he stood, a tall man, slightly stooped now, but with long black hair tinged with silver. He wore it tied, down his back. He strode to her.

"Cami."

"Yes, Great Uncle Clarence, thank you for meeting me."

They shook hands. He escorted her to a booth.

"What to drink?"

"Just coffee for me, black."

Her uncle ordered. After their first cup, they added pie to their next order. She liked listening to his accent; he still spoke his language, plus she heard a French twist in several English words he spoke.

"My Aunt Bea's never really talked about her family. I'm just so happy that she researched, finding you. It's kinda a miracle. That sorta happened to me with my mom's folks, kinda discovered them after mom and dad died. So this completes knowing about my family, getting to know you."

At her request, Clarence drove her to the reservation, where she could view where he lived, where her Ohay grandparents grew up. His son, Robert, worked, so she was not able to meet him.

On the way back to her car at the café she thanked him for taking her. She learned that he spent his career as the caretaker of the elementary school on the reservation.

"I can pretty much fix any kind of problem, electrical, plumbing. Maybe you get some of your engineering skill from me."

"Granddad Ohay did surveying, maybe that counts in our family's science and math genes," Cami laughed with her uncle.

"Maybe," he paused and then began, "I'll be blunt, you know how your grandparents died, what happened to them?"

"I do, and it took Aunt Bea 10 years of Al-Anon meetings to recover from the effects of being raised in an extremely alcoholic family."

"I'll be in AA for the rest of my life."

"I'm sorry, I didn't know it'd affected you also."

"Our whole family, Cami; divorced my wife, she drank, dragged me down; I'm at fault, I also drank."

"I'm glad you're still getting help."

At Cami's request they drove to the Ohay family grave area. She took pictures of her grandparents' gravestones at Aunt Bea's special request. Bea came to her parents' funerals all those years ago, but never got to see their gravestones. As they stood there near her grandparents' graves, Clarence shared several stories of the family, living on the reservation for four generations. Cami remembered parts of a quote, from her dad, that he wrote in the front of the journal she kept growing up. It was a piece from Crowfoot, the great leader of the Blackfoot (Siksika).

"What stays with me is that life is a shadow running across the grass losing itself in the sunset."

"Ah, I've heard of that saying, Cami."

"I'll remember it always, a vivid visual."

He nodded to her as they headed back to Cami's car.

"Thank you for coming to meet me; it means a great deal that our family's gotten reconnected. I never dreamed that would happen. Good luck in your work with Benel in Edmonton. That's going to be an amazing project."

Cami raised her arms and hugged him. She waved as he watched her leave the café parking lot.

§Ɔ

"Winter in Edmonton meant bundling up in multiple layers of clothing," Cami shared with her family in warm and cozy Georgia.

"Will you get used to it?"

"Yup, 'cause I have to be outside in this, the planning can't go on forever. We have to get out and start constructing and deconstructing to bring the light rail in."

Bea shook her head as she heard her niece talk.

"Can you come?"

"Yeah, they're giving me a Friday and a Monday, since I'm the maid of honor."

"Bring your long black dress. That'll be perfect as your maid of honor dress. We'll be carrying red flowers."

"Father marrying you?"

"Right, we've gone through pre-nup stuff; glad we did, 'cause there's still so much we have to learn about each other."

"After all this time."

"That's right, Cami, especially what we think about children, and where we'll eventually live in Ephrine.

"Maybe somewhere out near the stables."

"Chet's renovating his home; it's beautiful the way it was, but he says he's updating plumbing, electrical. He's mentioned to us that he has a special wedding present for us."

"Uh huh, I've an idea about that, Aunt Bea."

"Gotta go; hey, you seeing anyone?"

"A fellow engineer on the project, just one date so far; Cole calls; we talk; one day at a time, dear auntie."

"Getting your career under control."

"Exactly."

&

The warmth of their love encompassed Cami as she stood near her aunt during the vows part of their ceremony. She felt the pound, pound of her heart as her mind took her back through Bea and their years together.

"I want what Bea and Jake have; God help me find that," she whispered as she walked down the aisle behind her aunt at the ceremony conclusion.

Chet gave Jake and Bea a reception at a smaller room in the country club. He mentioned to them that they were combining two households, so would have enough stuff. The reception filled his desire to honor them as they joined their lives together.

Cami paid attention at the reception to her aunt and how she held her own with the lawyers and wives from the firm for which she worked. And the stable families, they came to wish Jake and Bea well in their futures. Cami enjoyed their down home charm, something about being with the horses, special warmth, she decided.

℅

For three days after she returned to the snow and cold of Edmonton, she felt stiff. She decided her body didn't like the return from warmth to frigid conditions. Like thousands of other Edmontonians she rode the light rail train from her studio apartment to the Benel office downtown.

"It's so much easier than driving my car," she shared with fellow riders. She looked forward to seeing Mitch's sunny smile as he rode the train each day. He got on one station after she got on.

"We'll be out in it, today. You have your Arctic gear?"

"Uh huh, at work, keep it there," she looked up to this tall member of her LRT team.

They got off the train and made their way to their building. Later that day the team walked through the downtown core area where the new portion of the train and its track would weave, from Mill Wood to 102nd Street. Their laptop provided images of the track, in small sections. The entire project would add three kilometers to the already existing train track. Homesickness, for Georgia, and her family caught her up in February.

℘

"Cami, I want to come see you."

"Cole, hey it's good to hear from you. I was home; Bea and Jake married."

"Wow, I'm glad to hear that; theirs is a wonderful love. Will you be around the next few weeks?"

"Oh yeah, our project's ratcheting up, really exciting."

"Work weekends?"

"Nope, that's super different for me. I explore Edmonton, trails in the snow, so I hike like that."

Two Fridays later Cami stood, tiring of the three computer screens in front of her. She gazed out the window at the Edmonton skyline.

"Knock, knock," she heard a voice. She smiled as she turned. Her whole floor consisted of cubicles, no real walls between anything, just low partitions. Cami put her hands on the sides of her face.

"It's me."

She stood, dumbfounded.

"Cole!"

She moved to him, hugging him. He held her close, then kissed her cheek. Cami realized that everyone in the nearby cubbies could see this tall couple in their embrace. She stepped back from him and removed a packet from a chair.

"Please, sit."

Cole smiled to her and nodded, "You're still in shock. Yeah, I had a chance to get away, lucky to catch a non-stop to Edmonton."

"You're staying?" she questioned him.

"Uh huh, just for the weekend, catching a red-eye late Sunday night back to Atlanta; got a hotel room for two nights; I'm checked in there."

"I had a quiet weekend planned, a movie I wanted to see. And I'm kinda involved in a singles group at church."

"You still go to early service on Sunday?"

"Uh huh, I ride light rail nearly everywhere; wanta see what Benel is doing?"

"Absolutely, I gotta see what your work life is like."

"Lots of movement," she smiled to him. "And right now I can't seem to keep my heart from flipping around, seeing you, so much emotion."

"Yup," he nodded to her. "I could die in the pool of her eyes," his mind spun.

They agreed to meet in the first floor lobby after work. Cami took him to one of the only bars she knew, near work, the rail line close by.   They drank beers, ate the delicious hamburgers for which the pub got known, and they cried together.

"Losing someone you love, oh Cole, you know, I understand what that's like. I'll always have my folks with me." She put her hand on his arm as they sat across from each other, deciding on dessert. "Things about your lady, Hope, will stay with you, just like stuff about Greg'll stay with me. You'll forget about the bad stuff, and remember all the good stuff."

"I'm on the rebound; actually went out on a blind date. A guy from work suggested I meet this lady. And, well, it's too soon to meet a new someone. I'm so happy when I'm with you, Cami."

"Old friends, good memories, I'm happy," she nodded to him.

They talked, over coffee as the pub got quieter, the families going home. She gave him directions to her place.

"Come over after you get up. I'll fix us a big breakfast and we'll plan our day."

"Great, I'm weary."

They hailed a taxi. Cole insisted that Cami go home first, then he would get off at his hotel.

"Have a good night," he smiled to her and kissed her cheek.

"Until morning," she nodded to him as she got out in front of her apartment building.

ঞ

Cami rose early and went for a walk in her neighborhood.

"Goodness, this beautiful snow from two days ago still looks fresh, no wind and few footprints outside the sidewalks," she murmured as she walked along.   She showered when she returned. Cami surveyed the contents of her refrigerator and decided she could fix them a hearty breakfast, finishing off with cinnamon rolls she baked and froze earlier.

They hugged after she ushered him in. She put his coat in the closet.

"It's nice, bigger than I expected it to be, but about the size of my studio in Atlanta."

"Yeah, a nice-size, check it out, this bookcase piece pulls out into a Murphy bed."

"That's what it is, there's no bed out during the day."

"Cole," she raised her arms to hug him.

"Cami," he held her close, "I can never hold you enough."

He stepped back from her.

"I see you, in every tall blonde guy, at work, everywhere. I love you, Cole. I am so glad you came."

He took her hand, "I love you, that love keeps growing, year after year, gobsmacked for you, I think since I was 11."

"When you gave me the angel ornament that Christmas."

"I did."

"Oh, Cole."

He stopped her with a kiss. She kissed him back; the smoldering burn she felt for him flashed from her throat down through her groin area. They undressed each other, taking their time, touching and caressing, kissing and stroking.

Together they pulled down the bed. He came around, picked her up and lay her gently on the mattress.

"We've been waiting, our whole lives," she whispered.

He covered her mouth with kisses as she stroked his back, kneading his buttocks, close, close to her body. She arched her back, readying for him. Cole entered her slick moistness and together they rocked into each other. Cami felt the thrusting of Cole and the response of her heated vagina. They crushed into each other, Cami murmuring, "Cole, Cole," as they rode their orgasms together.

In the quiet they heard their hearts pounding and their breathing labored.

"You're incredible."

"And so are you."

They lay on their sides, looking into each other's eyes.

"Your eyes, to die for, Cami, bright green now."

"And your eyes, that baby blue, your happy eyes."

They caressed each other's bodies. When their wanting simmered, they came together, this time quieter, cherishing the feel of their bodies with their hands.

"Making love with you, I'm home, Cami, I'm home."

"Our search for this love of our lives, it's been a winding road, Cole."

"You found me."

"I have."

Later they busied themselves in the tiny kitchen area.

"Remember, I did the eggs, scrambled, those years ago."

"And I'm doing the bacon, like back then, microwaved."

They sat close as they devoured brunch. And they planned the rest of their day. They rode the light rail to the Benel construction area for the expansion of the train. Cami walked him through the area that they were allowed to be in, explaining the process by which the rail line would go in.

"Amazing, truly, Cami, I admire you and all constructors so much, to figure this all out."

She kissed him on the cheek before they walked away from the site.

"But, oh, my dear, we must still have our financial folks, the monies we gotta have to create this thing."

"So, are you saying accountants are important?"

"Exactly."

The rest of that day they talked, went to dinner, and planned times when they could meet each other during the next few months.

"A long distance relationship, it'll be tough, Cami."

"We can do it; besides, you're still in rebound, and for me it's all new. We need the time. And time for our love to discover its bounds."

"If there are any bounds, there is so much to learn about you. We were just such kids in college. This's the real world out here, opening our hearts to each other and to other folks."

ℰꙩ

Cami felt a sharp pain of anguish, like a small tear in her heart, when she said goodbye as the taxi picked Cole up for his ride to the airport. She recalled this day, every detail.

They promised each other to stay in touch by e-mail and a phone call twice a week. Cole asked her to marry him, as they stood outside of church after mass on Sunday morning.

"I will marry you."

She smiled up into his eyes, and nodded, "God's with us, truly, right here, right now."

"His will be done, on earth, in heaven."

Cami felt, for the next months, like she raced against a timeclock, in her personal as well as her professional life. The light rail project progressed at an amazing pace. She learned that she would be transferred by Thanksgiving, to the Benel office in Oak Ridge, TN. Cole finished his first year with the State. He moved on, finding a federal government accounting job in Oak Ridge. After Thanksgiving and her transfer Cami joined him.

"This's gonna take some getting used to, Cami, dear girl. It's been awhile since I've lived with another person."

"Yup," she kissed him, stepped away, and then came back and kissed him again. "Kisses, many kisses, every day, that's what I want."

They hugged as he commented, "Hey, it'll be hard getting anything done if we keep this up."

They laughed together. Within a few hours of working with her possessions Cami felt confident she was as moved in as she could be.

"You don't have much stuff, Cami."

"Minimalist."

"For sure."

Their first night Cami fixed mac and cheese, salad, and, at Cole's special request, cheese cake. They drank champagne, to celebrate beginning their lives together.

"Thanks to Father Francis, we know each other better."

"Yeah, Father asked tough questions in the paperwork he sent us to fill out."

"And thanks to Skype, we got to talk with him in person, about who we are, who we think we are to each other, what we want together for the rest of our lives, and our desire for children."

Cole shook his head, "Did you have a hard time answering some of the questions as we got ready to talk to him by Skype?"

"Course, things I'd never really thought about, and then to have to speak everything out, for Father to hear."

They took their coffee to the couch in front of the fireplace.

"Father thinks we're ready to join our lives together; uh, we're kinda getting a head start, being together for several weeks before we marry."

"Cami, it's really important to find out," he paused, "what we're like, when stress surrounds us, like the assignment I'm on now. I'm kinda quiet when I'm stressed."

"And so am I, a lot on my mind, makes me silent, my mind working hard."

Cole set their glasses aside and guided her head to his chest.

"Can't believe how organized you've been about the wedding, simple, at that crazy time between Christmas and

New Year's. And to have a quiet little catered reception in the living and dining rooms of the B&B, not far from St. Luke's. 'Cause, Cami," he paused, "we don't know a lot of folks from home any more, and with new jobs, we just haven't had time to develop friendships here."

"Yeah, my friends in Edmonton, too far to come. But Justine'll be able to be here. And Indella, and your folks, and grandparents, Bea and Jake, and Chet. All the folks we love, for so long. And Cole, my parents seem close to me again, think about them some, again, seeing them in several couples I've run into in the past. Cole, I don't know anyone to ask how I look, so, I know it's not the way it's usually done, but could you come with me when I get my wedding dress?"

"Course, everything about what we're doing, it's a little quirky, that's OK. And you don't have an engagement ring, at your request. So we need to look at what we want for wedding rings."

"I want a wide gold band, yeah, I know that silver, platinum, is the look now, but not for me, I love gold, warm," she raised her head from his chest and smiled to him.

⁊〇

"It'll be two days after Christmas," they shared in their calls.

They did not send out wedding announcements, just told their friends and families the time and location in Ephrine.

Cami spent her second night home with Bea and Jake.

"My last time, this coming home, as a single person, I'm so happy, Bea," she shared with her aunt as they sat across from each other at the kitchen island.

Bea reached across and touched Cami's hand.

"You're such a giving person, Cami, when I look at you, I feel so grateful, you gave me my life, a part of you became a part of me."

"Justine's gonna join us in a little while; I just wanted the two of you with me for a little bachelorette celebration, at our favorite café."

"What'll Cole do?"

"Out with his dad and an uncle for a little while. His one friend left in town is on an assignment and can't get home."

On her wedding morning Cami got to the church a little early. She wanted time to be by herself. Cole peeked into this room where they all would meet right before.

"Justine's not here yet to do her maid of honor stuff. So I'm sharing, Cami, oh Cami, I'm so excited."

He held her hands in his.

"Cole, this's a surprise," she watched his eyes beam to her. "I gotta say this, 'cause I'll not remember, oh Cole, being with you, it grows sweeter and sweeter every day."

"And life, our life, wherever it takes us, your embrace, it'll always be my home. And your smile, your love, it's warmth and comfort."

They hugged and held on tight.

"We'll share soon, our vows, for forever, the rest of our lives."

℅

She felt them, next to her, with Chet on her other side. They stood in the aisle, at St. Luke's, waiting for the song prompt from the pianist at the grand piano.

"Mom and Dad, thank you for watching over me, you guys, and God," she thought as tears formed in her eyes.

Chet saw that and whispered, "You OK?"

She turned to him, "Overwhelmed, loved."

"Deep breaths."

The mass, and the vows, time accelerated. That's what Cami expressed as she and Cole cut the cake together.

"Come back for seconds," Cole spoke out to the group.

"Yeah, everybody in this bunch has a sweet tooth," Chet exclaimed, as they all laughed. Champagne punch and fudge rounded out the goodies.

Cami and Cole said their goodbyes to their invited guests after good wishes went around to all, and Happy New Year's also. They spent the night there at the B&B and returned to Oak Ridge. They both had to return to work right away after the New Year.

ༀ

They found a trail not far from where they lived. On Sundays, after mass, they brought sandwiches and drinks for their trail hike. When they got hungry, they stopped for lunch. The sunlight caught them as they sat on a rock off the trail. Cole kissed her cheek after she took a bite of the pb&j.

"Every day, I learn more about you, and every day, I love you more."

"Oh Cole, I love you, more each day. It's gonna be amazing, our lives, headed in many directions with my work. And you, willing to follow on, wherever I head."

They moved closer to each other and hugged.

"Our love," they whispered to each other.

CASTLE IN THE AIR

Fourteen-year-old best friends, Dee and Lana, give up their castle and imaginary prince charming for real boys who like them a lot. Both teens have jobs, home responsibilities, and school work. The talented young women love to sing and perform at school and other events. Lana's momma dies, and Dee's body revolts in a series of illnesses that keep her from school for many weeks. Troy is Lana's special guy. Dee and Lana have a fun summer together before their sophomore year. Lana becomes pregnant after her first sexual encounter with Troy. Dee and Michael care for each other. They realize that friendship is all their relationship can be at this time. What looms ahead for them is Dee's desire for her university degree and Michael's desire for both his degree and his military commission if he does get admitted to West Point. Dee and Michael date, go on a family ski trip, attend Prom, and spend time together.

Troy and Lana decide to marry. Lana and her dad move her from her home in Kansas to Iowa where Troy now lives. Lana changes her mind and does not marry Troy. She stays with Troy's aunt and uncle and finishes her sophomore year of high school and prepares for her GED exam. She plans to take the exam before her baby is due in July. Lana works weekends as a waitress. Dee and Lana continue their friendship by writing and calling each other.

Lana sings, lending her soprano voice to her high school choir. Troy graduates, and with a draft number of four in his Iowa county he decides to sign up for the Army. He wants to be a medic. He asks Lana to marry him. She is now more determined than ever to go it alone. While waitressing Lana meets Jeff who is studying for his bar exam in Iowa. They become friends. David is born soon after she completes and passes her GED. David becomes her reason for living, a part of Troy who will remain with her. As she always planned, Lana wants a career in the health field. She trains to be an X-ray technician after she completes several required classes at a junior college where she also works. While in training Lana is asked to sing at a hospital foundation talent show.

Senior year is difficult for both Dee and Michael as they see a time out coming in their relationship. They take a choral class together. Michael always wanted to be part of a singing group, and every day he gets to hear Dee's voice. They are special friends who share memorable moments at Senior Prom and their high school graduations.

As Dee promises, she visits Lana in Iowa, and they spend a nostalgic weekend together. They will continue to write and call each other. Dee and Lana wish each other safe journeys in the next phase of their lives.

Lana completes her training program and spends a somewhat frantic summer applying for jobs in her field. Troy finishes his two years of duty, the last one spent in Vietnam as a medic. He gets malaria at the end of his tour and is hospitalized. He returns to Grand Valley and sees David for the first time. Again he asks and is rejected in his desire to marry Lana. Lana and David move on; she has an X-ray technician position at a medical center at the University of Iowa. She says goodbye to Troy, and to Jeff.

Dee and Michael part at their high school graduation. Their love endears them to each other. Dee continues her summer bank job, and Michael enters West Point. Dee and her friend, Lindy, sing one time with a country band. Dee meets a guy in the band. He asks her out. They date twice; Kent knows of her plans and urges her to never stop singing. He appreciates her musical talent and wonderful voice. She dances almost every weekend with Michael's friend, Ben. Fall semester Dee and Ben attend Kansas State University.

ABOUT CATHLEEN

WWW.CATHLEENELLIS.COM

Cathleen Ellis is a Colorado native. She and her husband, John, live in the northern part of the state. They have four sons, three daughters-in-law, and four grandchildren. Cathleen draws the inspiration for her love stories from the lives of young people with whom she has lived and worked her entire life.